spirits
at the dawn
of day

We each contain the spiritual gifts that can help manifest a new harmonious age for humanity. The choice to illuminate them is yours. The paths we can choose to do this are numerous but the destination of enlightenment remains the same. May my words provide you with guidance on your path.

spirits at the dawn of day

simon boylan

OMNISCIENT
DOORWAYS

OMNISCIENT
DOORWAYS

© Omniscient Doorways
omniscientdoorways.com
Melbourne, Victoria 3000 Australia
simonboylan.com

Text copyright © Simon Boylan 2013

First published 2013 by
© Omniscient Doorways

Printed by Amazon USA
Cover & Book design by Brad Maxwell
Relevant reprint information, legal notices or other info on the book as required

simon boylan

spirits
at the dawn
of day

chapter 1

The vast, interconnected web pulsed before him. His vantage point allowed him to see most of the city while he took a short break from his meeting. His business associates were finalizing the proposal he had travelled to deliver, allowing him time to sip his Chai Latte and observe the mighty expanse that is modern Tokyo.

Josh's frequent visits to Japan were always pleasurable. His love of technology had provided him with the financial success to pursue his other love, Japanese women. He was captivated by their refined, elegant beauty and adored being around them.

Josh owned a company concerned with finding and importing innovative high end Japanese technology to Australia and the United States. He was currently standing on the 23rd floor of a skyscraper located in the business district of Shinjuku West. Hiroyuki Takahashi, the Managing Director and owner of Takahashi Consumer Electronics was taking a final look over the contractual documents that he and Josh had come to agreement on over the previous two days.

Mr. Takahashi's meticulous attention to every detail of his life was as evident in his final contract analysis as it was with the detail in which he formed his appearance. His was a regal presentation. Neatly combed grey hair sat atop an ageless face, largely thanks to genetic gifts from his Japanese forefathers. His eyes were framed with thin wire spectacles and he was dressed in an immaculate blue pin-striped three piece Armani suit with Prada shoes.

Mr. Takahashi presented a significant contrast to Josh. Similarly dressed in Armani, his was a slightly disheveled appearance; a permanent five o'clock shadow adorned his angular jaw line, with hair product holding in place his messed but styled black hair. His two piece suit was black, covering a silk white shirt unbuttoned at the collar, minus the constriction of a tie. Josh was alone in Japan, not feeling the need of having his own set of lawyersor associates accompany him for such an important deal.

Filled with a supreme confidence that seemed to permeate every aspect of his life, he *knew* he didn't need anyone else. He seldom does. In the world of business Josh had found his niche in life, somewhere he could display the intellectual and social talents he had cultivated and reap the rewards monetary success brings.

Mr. Takahashi's hand moved across the antique desk to grasp his fountain pen. Finally satisfied with the contract, he signed it quickly, cementing their relationship for the next five years. Josh walked over to stand in front of his desk and delivered a bow in respect.

"Arigatoo gozaimasu," he said, thanking him in the little Japanese he spoke.

"Doo itashimashite," Mr. Takahashi replied, extending a deep bow himself. He then offered his hand in the traditionally western gesture. They shook hands, exchanged some final pleasantries and Josh was soon on his way out of the office.

As he walked out into the foyer he was farewelled with a bow by Mr. Takahashi's personal assistant, Yuki Nakamura. A stunning girl with a porcelain face, straight shoulder length jet black hair and a perfectly proportioned physique, her hands were clasped in front of her as she rose from her bow. Her right index finger nervously stroked the wedding band on her left hand as both she and Josh experienced a brief mental flashback of their shared sexual escapade from the previous night.

Josh bowed in return and thanked her, unable to contain the smile that arose when thinking of his gorgeous conquest. He had effectively compartmentalized any traces of guilt that were still present in him, contained as they had been the previous night. With obvious remorse from Yuki, it seemed she didn't share this talent.

The ability to circumvent the moral compass, the conscience, was an ability that Josh had honed increasingly over the last decade. It was the same skill that enabled ordinary people to do the most horrendous things. The majority of people had some aptitude for this in their lives, employed when their immediate desires overpowered thoughts of what they *should* be doing. Josh believed he had mastered this ability and applied it whenever required by the situation, locking any cumbersome feelings of remorse and guilt deep within the recesses of his subconscious. Josh didn't consider himself to be a bad person. After all, he hadn't killed anyone, and nor would he. He just didn't see any problem with the manipulation of others for his own material gain.

Everyone was free to choose what they did in this life, and if those choices could be influenced to benefit him through some subtle, or not so subtle language of persuasion, he felt compelled to do so. After all, he thought, what else was there?

He made his way to the nearest elevator and was soon in a taxi travelling to the airport. While passively taking in the blur of life from the passing streets his phone began to vibrate. Retrieving it from his left breast pocket he found Kush Raymore waiting to talk.

"Mr. Tokyo! How'd it all go?" Kush asked.

"How do you think, my friend?" Josh replied. "Mr. Takahashi loves me. The contracts were locked in about an hour ago."

"Nice. And the ladies?" Kush probed.

"What makes you think there were ladies? I've only been here two days!"

"Cut the shit Josh. It's me man!"

"Well, there was this one girl..."

Kush let out a loud burst of laughter. "And?"

"Gorgeous. The face of an angel."

"They always are. So you banged her?"

Josh sighed. "Yes, Kush, in your crude vernacular, I banged her."

The taxi made a sharp right turn causing Josh to drop his left hand to the seat to brace himself. The taxi driver waved his hand in apology.

Kush raised his voice, "Nice!"

"But there was one small problem. She was kind of married..."

"Ouch, Josh. So you've left another sorry bastard out there with a cheating wife."

Josh didn't reply.

"Fuck it man. Can't be too happy at home if she's out sleeping with *gaijin* as they step off the plane!"

"Yeah, I guess you're right."

"Of course I'm right! Now cut this sorry shit and get your ass back here so we can celebrate this victory properly!"

"Sure. I'll see you soon."

Josh hung up his phone, replaced it in his pocket and settled back into his head. Slightly agitated by fresh thoughts of the previous night's marital infidelity, he forced his attention back to his surroundings. As apartment blocks slowly became fields, an abundance of grey was replaced with rich, vibrant greens as he observed the gradual transition from urban to rural landscapes. Lush farmland filling the taxi's windows signaled Josh's imminent arrival at Narita Airport.

Josh arrived at the check-in counter to discover there had been a mistake with his reservation. All business class seats had been allocated, with only one economy seat left on the fully booked plane.

"Let me get this straight…" Josh asked the customer service agent, "…you have taken more reservations than you have seats on the plane?"

"Apparently sir." the agent replied.

Josh clenched his fist as anger began to animate his face.

"But why? How can this happen?"

"I don't know, sir. I do apologize. There must have been some error in our system. We are flying at full capacity."

"I see that. If you weren't, you'd have a seat for me!" he yelled.

"Again, I do apologize sir, but there's nothing more I can do. You can either take the remaining seat, or stay in a hotel with our compliments and fly out tomorrow."

"These are the options you give me? Either ride in the extreme discomfort of fully booked cattle class or screw up my schedule for a week by arriving a day late!"

"I'm sorry, sir, there is nothing more I can do. Of course you will be compensated if you decide to take the economy seat."

"You're damn right. But we'll leave the compensation discussion for later."

He felt the outside of his jacket pocket to confirm the presence of his sleeping pills.

"I'd better be served business class meals!" Josh stated, pointing his finger at the representative.

"Again, I do apologize, sir", the attendant said as he handed over Josh's boarding pass. Josh snatched it and stormed off in silence. He quickly made his way through the various security checkpoints and passport control, proceeding without further incident. Josh then found the nearest bar in an effort to quell his seething rage and start the process of anesthesia for the trip ahead. After 15 minutes and three shots of bourbon, he was sufficiently sedated by the time his flight was ready to leave.

Slightly inebriated, he slowly followed the direction of the last call for his flight, making his way to the departure gate. With all his fellow passengers already on the plane, he quickly made his final check-in and was soon at the entry door to the aircraft.

Waiting at the entrance to check his boarding pass for the last time was flight attendant Makiko Yamamitsu, a beautiful Japanese woman in her mid-thirties. She greeted him with a perfect British accent, a bow and a smile.

"Good evening sir." she said.

Any lingering anger present from his ticketing mix-up momentarily vanished as he had to stop himself from staring. Her long black hair was wrapped up in a tight bun behind her head, with subtle make up coloring her face.

"Uh...good evening." Josh replied, handing her his boarding pass.

"Thank you. You're seated in seat 64H. Please move down this aisle."

She motioned toward the aisle behind her.

"Thank you." Josh replied, still unable to avert his gaze.

"You're welcome sir. Enjoy your flight." she said, bowing her head.

Josh brushed past Makiko as he made his way towards the aisle, lightly touching her forearm with his hand and capturing a hint of her Christian Dior perfume.

Glancing at her name tag and making a mental note of her name for use in any later game of seduction, he proceeded down the aisle as instructed. He came first to business class. He had not previously realized how taunting this forced journey could be. Everyone seated in the lower class was subjected to the compulsory tour of how one would travel if they'd done just a little bit better in life, tried a bit harder or been a bit smarter. As Josh walked through, those fortunate few already seated here averted their gaze in an unconscious attempt to avoid corruption, or be reminded of where he was headed. He had the ridiculous impulse to call out that it was all a mistake... that he was indeed one of them... but just as soon as the thought had arisen he had already moved through their world and into the other.

Josh hadn't travelled economy for years, but it seemed far worse than he had remembered it. Movement to his seat was obstructed by those trying to cram their tightly packed bags into the overhead compartments. To his right he could see an argument unfolding between an older passenger and a flight attendant. She was trying to tell him that his bag must be placed in the overhead compartment, but he would not listen. The mildly obese man with greying hair and thick brown glasses was becoming hysterical. The flight attendant looked on in disbelief, raising her hands in exasperation. At an impasse, she was soon forced to issue him with the ultimatum of either placing the bag overhead or leaving the plane. After this threat he finally consented, to a look of relief of all nearby witnessing the scene. It was clear to Josh that it was going to be a long flight.

He continued down the cramped aisle, holding his carryon luggage above his head to avoid getting caught in the legs and arms frustrating his path. People were literally bursting out of their seats wherever he looked, either due to their natural size or the western proclivity of eating ones way through the many tribulations of life. Mild claustrophobia was taking hold. Josh wanted to change his mind and get off the squashed aircraft, but it was already too late.

Josh was unaware he only had to shift his perception slightly to witness a very different scene. The emotional turmoil of frustration and dread the he carried with him compelled him to focus on the people and scenes that would help reinforce these negative mental states.

He missed the majority of people on the aircraft who were excited about their trip, all eager to be there. Not considering their uncomfortable surrounds, they were at one with the thought, 'I'm going overseas! I'm going to Australia!' The enthusiasm of many was palpable on the plane, but this all flowed around him, with only negativity becoming part of his immediate world view.

Finally arriving at his seat, Josh attempted to stow his carryon luggage above him. But, because of his late arrival, all nearby compartments were full. A flight attendant recognized his plight and came over to assist him, taking his bags and finding a place for them. Josh was relieved to finally be able to sit down, despite his cramped surroundings. He was seated beside a young Japanese couple in their mid-twenties, both acknowledging his presence with a polite bow of their heads which Josh reciprocated. As he was one of the last to board, the plane taxied for departure and took off not long after he was seated.

Eager to forget the experiences of the past hour, Josh immediately popped some Temazepam to help him fall asleep. Sinking into his chair, he was quick to succumb to the chemically induced slumber. After the passing of a few hours, he was gently woken by the couple sitting next to him, both wanting to get out and use the restroom. Following numerous apologies and head bows from the pair, he grumbled acknowledgement of their request and stood up, stumbling to his feet in a slightly groggy, drugged hangover.

Waiting for the couple to return, Josh remained standing, placing his hand over his mouth and releasing a protracted yawn. Tilting his head to the side as he looked around the plane, he sighed with relief as his neck released a forceful crack.

All window shutters had been closed and the cabin lights were set to a minimum, with the main luminescence derived from a scattering of screens still lit by people watching movies. The majority of the plane had fallen asleep. Eager to join them all again, he pressed the call button to request a glass of bourbon. The couple returned as the flight attendant delivered his drink, allowing him to settle in again. He threw back another couple of pills and washed it down with the sweet American liquor. He let out a loud sigh and closed his eyes, with sleep quickly finding him again.

Hours again passed with Josh oblivious to his surroundings. His unconsciousness was shaken with the sound of a loud bang and the plane suddenly losing altitude. There was a concordant gasp across the cabin. The wave of fear settled then quickly dissipated when there was no escalation. The plane hummed with voices all discussing the sudden fears that were aroused. The talk was punctuated with nervous laughter. Josh, still groggy from his drugged sleep, let out a loud yawn as he stretched his arms above his head. The young couple beside him were holding hands, the girl again nestling into her partners shoulder. Josh smiled.

A small vibration that had permeated the cabin began to escalate. The seat-belt light began to flash and a nervous energy again spread amongst the passengers. Panic grew with the increasing intensity of the vibration. Josh buckled his seat belt, gripped his arm rests and chuckled to himself.

"With the amount of daily air travel going on, there is no way I would be so unlucky to be on one that crashed! Especially flying a reputable airline, the chances of that happening are next to none!" Josh thought.

His reassuring internal dialogue was offset by the increasing movement of his seat. Handgrips tightened as everyone was increasingly shaken. A tenuous calm then descended over the cabin as the vibration suddenly vanished. Few had the courage to let go of their seats, all frozen in the hope it was over, all wondering what was going to happen next. This question was soon answered with the noise of an explosion from the right side of the plane.

The sound of the blast tore through the aircraft. An orange haze beamed through nearby windows, illuminating the environment in a maniacal dance of shadow and light. Panic gripped the entire plane but true chaos unfolded when one passenger shrieked:

"TERRORISTU!"

Infected with hysteria, the passengers' screams cried out above all other noise.

Fire consumed the right engine. The plane banked right and began rapidly losing altitude. Josh sat in a state of shock, a stunned silence.

The drastic course change sent luggage flying through the air. Dislodged bags careered into people. A heavy briefcase crushed a passenger's eye socket. Emergency lights flickered on. Oxygen masks appeared from the ceiling, flailing back and forth.

Josh remained in a catatonic state, overcome by fear, only able to bear witness to the madness that surrounded him. He watched as loved ones held each other in tears. The couple next to him were wrapped in each other's arms. The young man's lips rested on his partner's ear, quietly singing a song and softly stroking her head. Others were screaming uncontrollably. One hysterical passenger was making his way up the aisle in a futile attempt to escape.

Some had their hands clasped in prayer, asking for a safe return to their loved ones. Others accepted their impending death and were asking for a smooth transition to the afterlife.

Josh didn't have anything to turn to, having ridiculed any religious or spiritual belief for most of his adult existence. He could never see any rational explanation for why one would be religious, believe in the essentially unprovable... have *faith*? Finally he was presented with an answer. Faith in a higher power may provide you with some peace in your final moments. Could it be that a lifetime of religious practice and devotion may finally bear fruit?

Paralyzed by the fear of his imminent death, he also appreciated what may prompt a deathbed conversion, a final plea for one's soul. However, he was again excluded from this. Any such conversion would require a tacit religious belief all along, akin to a petulant child who would not acknowledge their father's authority until he found themselves in a dire predicament requiring it. As no such belief had been cultivated, any conversion would be a lie. In the remote chance that God *did* exist, he would of course realize this lie through his omniscience and Josh would still be banished to the same fiery nether region for all eternity.

He looked down at his own empty hand. With no one to hold on to and no God promising salvation, he could not escape the conclusion that he was all alone in this world. He had a girlfriend of sorts back home and a number of other women that he could call on if he felt the need, but in that moment he realized the futility of all of his relationships up until that point of his life. Concentrating on the superficialities in life in an effort to avoid emotional trauma, the crushing emptiness of this path was all too apparent as he neared his death.

Racking his brain for someone with whom he had connected, someone who he would like to be with during his final moments, Elizabeth finally revealed herself to his mind's eye. She had been so effectively repressed by his mechanisms of denial and avoidance that he had literally not given her a single thought in over eight years. Now with the specter of death apparent, tears flowed down his face together with thoughts of the love that he had lost. At that moment Josh viewed many of those around him as lucky... lucky since they have their loved ones to accompany them in their remaining minutes.

These resurrected thoughts of Elizabeth actually made his impending death harder to face. Any ponderings of a wasted life were too much for his now terrified mind. He began to breathe heavily and tried again to focus on his surroundings. He would find no solace there. The screams had not abated. His fellow passengers were all painfully aware of their role as helpless occupants of the falling plane.

Cans of drink rolled back and forth down the aisles and under the seats as the plane lurched violently from side to side. Down his aisle he could see Makiko valiantly struggling to make her way up the plane, attending to passengers as she went. Josh looked to his left and a strange sight caught his eye.

Another petrified couple were sitting next to him in the center section, both shivering and huddled over each other. They were slumped down in their seat, allowing Josh to see the man sitting next to them. In contrast to the twisted, terrified faces that surrounded him, this man was sitting with the calm of an enlightened monk.

Seemingly unaffected by their dire situation, he was sitting straight up in his seat with his eyes closed. His palms faced straight up in his lap, with his right hand resting on his left and his mouth shaped in a small, serene smile.

"What the hell's going on?" Josh thought. "How could he be happy?"

Looking more carefully Josh saw the man's smile did not reveal a perverse joy in their horrific conditions. It was more a reflection of his inner state. He was still somehow anchored in a place of peace. Josh couldn't stop staring; his presence was entirely incongruous with the circumstances that surrounded him.

He watched as the man took in a deep breath through his nose, his belly expanding as his lungs filled downwards.

As he released his breath in a long, slow exhalation, his eyes gradually drew open.

Josh suddenly felt a wave of peace... of compassion... move through him. These emotions somehow expanded throughout the plane.

Although totally ignorant of *how*, Josh *knew* the peaceful man was responsible. Sitting back in amazement, he watched as the pervasive screams began to die down. Everyone was being influenced by the man's benevolent intention. Soon the sound of gentle crying was the only human noise to be heard, quietly accompanying the clamor of the alarms and diseased mechanisms of their sick aircraft.

Observing this mysterious stranger, Josh had forgotten his surroundings and imminent death. All thoughts of fear and sadness had been consumed by the compassion that the man was able to manifest and then radiate. Josh could only sit back and stare in awe.

Now approaching Josh, Makiko the flight attendant was still heroically attempting to tend to passengers. She struggled to make her way up the aisle as she fitted people with life jackets. This task was made harder with dislodged luggage littering her path and catapulting towards her with every major movement of the plane. Looking up from securing a passenger's life jacket, she glimpsed a flash of silver from the chassis of a laptop just before it smashed into her forehead. Leaving her slightly concussed with blood streaming down her face from her wound, she grabbed a nearby armrest to steady her and pressed on, turning to Josh.

"We're going to crash. You need to put on a life jacket and brace yourself for impact." she shouted, wiping her brow of blood as it entered her eyes.

She reached down and grabbed a life jacket from beneath his seat, pulling it down over his head. It was at that moment that the calm stranger turned to meet Josh's eyes.

Makiko continued to yell instructions at Josh, grabbing his hand and placing it on the life jacket inflation cord. Josh looked on in silence, totally consumed by the gaze from the man across the aisle. She reached around and pulled the adjustment tab, securing the life jacket to Josh.

Now totally enveloped by the man's compassionate stare, Josh was at peace as the plane met the ocean surface and darkness descended upon them all.

chapter 2

At 4:50 AM on a Wednesday morning, Josh's awareness returned to the present moment. He could hear the soft beep of machines monitoring his vital signs as he opened his eyes to reveal the dimly lit hospital room in which he lay. Air moved between his parched lips as he took in a slow breath. His mind was only able to briefly register where he was before his awareness was to leave once again. One of the few to be discovered alive after the plane crash, he had been transferred by helicopter to the Alfred Hospital's emergency department in Melbourne, Australia.

While in care, his days were shrouded in a ubiquitous haze. Perpetually drifting from consciousness to sleep, the only words to imprint on his bruised mind were those that were parroted by everyone that entered his room. *"You are so lucky to be alive..."*

Apart from some minor cuts and bruises and a severe blow to the head, Josh had managed to come through his ordeal virtually unscathed. After his concussion had subsided and his conscious state had stabilized, his doctors were able to give him a clean bill of health and he was to be released in a matter of days.

Josh had lived through a surreal nightmare. So many questions were raised within him in such a short space of time, his body and mind seemed incapable of fully processing his experience. Buoyed by news of his hospital release, he was eager to get back home and return to some sense of normalcy.

Exiting the taxi from the hospital, Josh looked up at his building. A sleek, modern structure of metal and glass, his apartment was on the 23rd floor. Making his way through the foyer, he encountered one of his building's security staff.

"Mr. Black! So good to see you are alright. That was a horrible accident." he said.

"Yes, it was." Josh replied.

"Can I help you with anything?"

"I'm fine, thank you. I just want to get up to my apartment."

"Of course, sir. I'm sorry. Please let me know if there's anything I can do for you."

"Thanks."

Slightly embarrassed that he never bothered to remember the man's name after living there for two years, Josh quickly made his way into the elevator and up to his apartment.

Opening the door, he could see his apartment was as he left it. He took off his shoes, left them next to the large Peace Lily near the door and let out a large sigh. He was finally home. He expected some feeling of comfort upon his return but he had not found it. Josh wasn't sure about how he was expected to feel, but he didn't expect to feel like *this*. Shaking his head and laughing to himself that he was even asking such questions, he decided to have a shower and get changed into some fresh clothes.

Stepping out of his shower and putting on a dark blue Adidas tracksuit, he stood back and looked at his bedroom. A king sized bed adorned with a black and white quilt cover took up the majority of space in the room, with an early black and white Brett Whiteley nude painting hanging above his bed. Many conquests had occurred here, something that he had always been proud of, but it all now seemed like an empty achievement.

He left his bedroom and went into the main living area of his apartment. An open plan design, Italian black marble tiles were laid throughout the kitchen and dining areas with the sunken lounge covered in fine wool carpet. The kitchen was fully equipped with the latest Miele appliances, metal counter tops, and an array of white cupboards. All furniture pieces in his house were from Poliform, from the grey lounge suite, to the Millerighe crystal coffee table. He had the latest in entertainment equipment, with a sleek 70 inch Sony display panel adorning the wall in front of the lounge and a Bose lifestyle system providing audio to every corner of his house. As a result of his company's dealings in Japan, he even had two fully electronic toilets.

Walking around his apartment, he didn't feel that sense of normalcy, of *home*, that he had sought. His house seemed sterile, unfeeling. It did not feel like his home. The only thing that seemed to provide any life at all was his large Peace Lily.

A gift from a former lover, it was the only object of any real color in the entire apartment other than a sullen Vincent Fantauzzo portrait on the lounge room wall. He went and sat down on his lounge.

"What's wrong with me? Nothing has changed, so how can everything be so different?"

Despite his confused internal dialogue, he knew that he himself had clearly changed and thus, by definition, for him *everything* had changed. The perceptual faculties of his five senses still streamed the same data, the same familiar environments that he had so carefully created, but as the observer had undergone some shift in perspective, the same sensory landscape illustrated a vastly different picture. Where Josh once saw trendy and modern, he now saw cold and impersonal. What he once saw as a physical embodiment of him and all he stood for, he now saw only a vacuous attempt to be 'cool'. All he could see was designed to impress the next pretty young thing he could coax up into his lair, to have his nefarious way.

"WHAT IS WRONG WITH ME?" Josh screamed out internally in silent mental anguish.

All too much, yet unable to escape from the source of his problem, he decided to put his feet up, shut his eyes and listen to some music.

He hit random on his integrated media center and closed his eyes, sinking into the plush leather.

The random fall of ones and zeros decided his first track to be Pearl Jam's '*Present Tense*'.

He let out a deep breath as the slow guitar riff began and Eddie Vedder's baritone voice washed over him.

> *Do you see the way that tree bends?*
>
> *Does it inspire?*
>
> *Leaning out to catch the sun's rays*
>
> *A lesson to be applied*
>
> *Are you getting something out of this all-encompassing trip?*
>
> *You can spend your time alone, redigesting past regrets, oh*

Or you can come to terms and realize

You're the only one who can't forgive yourself, oh

Makes much more sense to live in the present tense.

He quickly sat up and stopped the music. Having never really listened to the lyrics of the song before, the words proved to be extremely unsettling to his current state of mind. Pearl Jam's pensive prescription would have to wait. Now at a total loss of what to do next, only one thing came to mind.

"I have to get to work."

With his life generally consumed by his career, Josh felt certain that the one thing that could surely ground him back in his life was his company. He quickly threw on a suit, made his way out of his apartment building and walked across the city center to his corporate offices. Even his home city of Melbourne seemed foreign to him as he walked. The people and places previously familiar to him just didn't seem *right*. Feeling he was rapidly losing grip on reality, Josh put on his sunglasses, put his head down and focused on the short journey at hand.

Pushing open the glass double doors of his offices, he was greeted with a welcome sight.

Familiarity.

Michelle was at reception as she had been for the past 18 months. He nodded his head in acknowledgement as he strode past her. She had short blonde cropped hair, large blue eyes and a petite frame. She was wearing a tight black shirt showcasing her ample breasts as was her style. Michelle clearly fitted Josh and Kush's female hiring criteria. Only just noticing Josh's return, her jaw dropped just as he walked out of view.

Making a couple of brief greetings to other surprised staff members, Josh arrived at his office. His personal assistant Sandra Littleton was busy working at her desk just outside his office door.

"Josh!" Sandra exclaimed. She jumped out from behind her desk and threw her arms around him, giving him a kiss on his cheek and squeezing him tightly.

"What are you doing here? We've been so worried! We were all *so* relieved when we found out you'd survived. And look! Barely a scratch! What are you doing here? You should be at home resting, really…"

Josh stood back to take a breath.

"Sandra, thanks. It's good to be back. And alive..."

"What are you doing here? You shouldn't be here. Let me call you a cab to take you home. Do you want me to give you a lift?"

Sandra had been Josh's PA for three years. Hiring her as a recent university graduate at 21 years old, she had satisfied his main criteria of typing at over a hundred words per minute and being utterly gorgeous. Her neatly cut brown hair framed a perfect face and her taut yoga body had convinced many men to believe in the adage of 'love at first sight'. It was pure luck that she happened to be an excellent employee and have a kind, caring heart. She had rebuffed her boss's advances at numerous staff functions as she would never date anyone she worked with yet had received significant pay increases in each of her evaluations due to her proficiency and incredible work ethic.

"Sandra, I'm fine, really. I was going crazy at home so I just wanted to stick my head in here and see what's happening. I probably won't stay long."

"You shouldn't. You should be resting. Can I get you anything?"

"No really, I'm fine. I just want to sit in my office for a while. Thanks."

He closed his office door behind him and sat down. His Herman Miller chair snugly supported his lumbar spine as he stretched his arms above his head and leaned back.

"Now this seems more normal. Time. Time is all I need," Josh thought, not fully believing his words but happy enough to accept the delusion if it would give him some peace. This peace would be short lived.

His office door suddenly burst open with the arrival of Kush.

"Josh! Man, what the hell are you doing here! Why didn't you tell me you were coming! I could have come and got you!"

"Hey, Kush. It's no problem. It was more of a spur of the moment thing..."

"Couldn't keep away, hey!" Kush reached over and slapped the top of his head. "It's great to have you back man. It wasn't the same without you and the ladies of this town have been crying out for your presence! When are we hitting it man? Tonight? You are back! Fuck, you look amazing!"

"Yeah, Kush, don't think that's going to happen just yet..."

"Yeah, okay man. I guess you don't fall out of the sky in a flaming wreckage every day, do you! It's cool, but I am ready to go when you are. Just what you need."

Any familiarity that he thought he felt had quickly vanished in the presence of his crude colleague.

"I am friends with this guy!" he thought. "What the hell is wrong with me? And him!"

Sandra appeared at his open door, knocking quietly.

"Excuse me Josh. I have Phil Williamson on line 5. He is asking to talk to someone regarding the warranty conditions on a shipment of product he received from us a couple of months ago. He's pretty upset."

Kush raised his hand. "Don't worry Joshy boy, I'll handle it."

He sat down on Josh's desk, reached over and picked up his phone.

"Phil! How are you? Kush Raymore here"

Kush nodded his head a couple of times. "Sure, sure, sure, of course we do..."

Kush looked over at Josh and rolled his eyes, masturbating the air with his hand.

"Phil. Phil. Phil. You signed the contract. Those were the conditions you agreed to."

Kush continued to nod his head.

"Well it doesn't matter if it's fair or not. YOU SIGNED THE FUCKING CONTRACT!"

"Well fuck you, too. And go on, bring on the courts, that'll be the worst mistake you'll ever make.

You count yourself lucky that all you have is a few hundred dodgy TV's. Take us to court and we'll dismantle you and your entire business enterprise!"

"Nice to talk to you too." Kush leant over and slammed down the phone.

"Woo hoo! Now I know why you're back, Joshy boy, you miss it, don't you? I should have let you take that call!"

"Maybe you should have. I think I could've handed it with a little more tact."

"Tact? Dude...that was Phil Williamson...PHIL WILLIAMSON. YOU were the one that got him to sign. You were the one that screwed him! We would have never moved all that product if it wasn't for good old Phil. Can't you remember mate, after you'd owned his ass we went out slamming Yeager bombs and ended up banging those French twins!"

Disgusted by this forced recollection, Josh was left speechless. The memories that he had accessed seemed to belong to another person.

"Was I really such an asshole?"

Kush stared at him waiting for a response, but Josh didn't have any response to give. The stilted silence quickly turned uncomfortable so he hastily excused himself and proceeded home.

"Was I really such an asshole?"

The question circled around and around in his mind. Josh didn't believe it was wrong to want to succeed and he had worked hard to get to where he was. Now, where was that exactly? A home full of shallow material possessions with little meaning and a string of relationships with beautiful women devoid of emotional commitment? Is this the place he had worked so hard to get to? Josh recognized that cumulative personality change happened to everyone. Events occurring over time and our reaction to them serve to mold our identity, ensuring that who we are today is not the same person that we will be one year, two years or ten years from now. But to what extent do we actually choose to create the person we become? The incremental nature of such change makes it impossible to highlight the decisions or particular circumstances that make us who we are today as opposed to who we were yesterday. Josh believed that he was happy. And what is happiness other than believing that one is happy?

But now, according to the Josh of today, pre-crash Josh was a sad, sorry individual, and post-crash Josh knew exactly the moment that he had changed... over a 15 minute period... as his plane came to rest in the Pacific Ocean, just off the Australian coast.

The dramatic personality shift within him felt like it was going to tear him apart, or possibly give him another chance.

Days passed with Josh dwelling in self-imposed isolation in his apartment. Josh developed some new loves in his life: television, Indian and Italian take out, and television. Lots of TV. The most important feature of his apartment had been so underappreciated! His massive screen had never had such a workout before. Now it was rarely turned off. He was yet to make it to his bed since his return from hospital, setting up permanent camp on his sofa.

The television proved to be an endless source of distraction from the troubling thoughts that continued to creep into his mind, against his will. Who would have known that his existential crisis could have so easily been postponed by focusing on reality TV contestants, all trying to outdo each other for their 15 minutes of glory!

Take out containers continued to build up around him in precariously stacked towers but he was beyond caring at this point. Before long however, even the TV proved unsettling. Josh started to become unnerved as it seemed, for a time that the TV could read his mind, subtly prodding his consciousness with uncomfortable questions. It often provided a program at just the right time to address a question that was nagging him, or brought him a spokesperson to bring up a question he was trying to avoid. The string of coincidences that seemed to be building between his mind and the programming of local television networks was impossible to ignore, but still completely nonsensical to him. Thus, he had no alternative but to disregard these synchronous events, desperately running from his emergent awareness.

Concentrating on the more vacuous forms of entertainment seemed to help his sought ignorance, but even the most puerile reality TV would occasionally offer a kernel of truth to remind him of what he was avoiding.

Two weeks after he had begun his TV marathon, his buzzer sounded. Strange, he thought, he wouldn't be making his dinner order for at least another hour. He grabbed his nearby white flannel robe and put it on over his blue t-shirt and Superman themed pajama bottoms. He pressed the button on his intercom.

"Hello?" Josh asked.

"Josh! Where have you been? Why haven't you called me?" the female voice shouted.

"Uh...Nadine. Hi" he replied, wincing at the sound of her voice.

"Yes, it's Nadine. Now buzz me up!"

Josh took his finger off the button, paused a moment, and reluctantly buzzed her up. He left his front door ajar so she could let herself in and reassumed his well-worn position in front of the TV.

The front door soon edged open with Nadine peering inside.

"Josh?" she called out, scanning the room for signs of life.

"Yeah, in here. Come in."

Seeing the piles of dishes in the kitchen from the door, Nadine apprehensively stepped into his apartment. She stopped at the top of the entrance to the lounge.

"Well?" Nadine asked, her hands firmly placed on her hips. She was a striking figure even when clearly angry, standing at over five foot ten inches tall. As a popular swimsuit model for the surf brand, *Billabong*, her athletic body was only upstaged by her stunning face. A brunette with long rolling hair, she stood before him in a fitted, low cut black dress with a look of fury detracting from her sea blue eyes.

"Well what?" Josh answered.

"Why haven't you called?" Nadine insisted.

"In fairness, Nadine, you haven't called either."

"Have you checked your phone?"

Josh lent over and grabbed his phone to find that he had a number of text messages awaiting him.

"I said called, Nadine, not texted. In case you were not aware, I was in a rather big accident."

"Of course I know. I've been worried sick. It's all I ever hear from anyone... 'How is Josh?' 'Is he okay?' 'Is there anything I can do?' How do you think it makes me feel when I can't answer these questions? I'm supposed to be your girlfriend!"

"You could have called... or come over..."

"I did come over. I'm here now, aren't I? And what about me, Josh? Did you ever stop to think about me? About how I might be feeling?"

"I'm sorry, Nadine. I've been having a bit of a crisis. I really don't feel like myself and I wasn't sure you'd understand."

"You're having a crisis! I am supposed to be in LA in three days for a photo shoot and I'm not sure I can fly anymore. Stefan is threatening to replace me with Jessica for the new December TV spot, my skin is awful and I'm starting to break out, and *I know* you have forgotten about the dinner party at the Johnston's tonight!"

Josh stared back blankly. He was sitting there silently listening, not surprised by her rant.

"Look Nadine, I'm sorry I haven't called and I'm sorry I forgot about the dinner party tonight, but as I said, I WAS IN A PLANE CRASH!"

Nadine crossed her arms.

"Well... this clearly isn't working, is it, Josh? I tried and tried *and tried* to be there for you, to be supportive, but I can't keep doing this. I need to think about me. About what I want and what I deserve. You clearly can't think about anyone but yourself. It's over Josh! Goodbye."

With that, she turned her head, throwing her hair to the side and stormed out of his apartment. As she reached the front door, she called back to him,

"And Josh, clean yourself up. You're a disgrace." With these parting words, she slammed his door.

Sitting back mentally digesting the whirlwind that was Nadine, Josh felt better than he had in days. Experiencing relief to be free of such a high maintenance relationship, he could actually understand why Nadine reacted the way she did. His accident had totally changed the rules of the game.

In the past, Josh was more than happy to play the attentive boyfriend when required, stroking Nadine's ego with praise and monetary attention. In return, Nadine was happy to play arm candy for the rich, successful businessman out on the town, and the sexual vixen in the bedroom. Now with Josh unable to fulfill his role, it was only natural that she would want to move on to greener pastures. There would be a line of men at her door before the night was out, if he wasn't already replaced days ago. Either way, it didn't matter to him. Without the intellectual capacity to decipher this new world he had found himself in, Josh would be totally incapable of providing ego support to such a fragile princess.

Unfortunately for Josh, any relief he felt from his breakup was again short lived as he soon resumed the emotional rollercoaster he had begun weeks earlier. He quickly appreciated that he was now totally alone for the first time in his adult life. He had always had some form of female companionship over the years, usually physical from his point of view, but still always some romantic female presence.

He was happy to be rid of the drain that was Nadine, but sitting there alone staring at the TV, the thought of real companionship seemed like a pleasant dream, not something to ever be realized. As his mind drifted back through the array of women he could remember being with over the years, his mind soon came to settle on Elizabeth.

With thoughts of Elizabeth reminding him of his emotional outburst on the plane, he did his best to control himself, trying to again suppress any feelings and images before they could rise up. Alone and unencumbered by distraction this proved impossible, with Josh finally unable to avoid memories of Elizabeth and the wonderful life he started to remember.

Josh had been waiting in line to enroll for his freshman year at university when he first saw her across the hall. He had just struck up a conversation with Zach Holtzman, a fellow freshman who had been standing beside him in line. Developing an immediate rapport with Zach, they talked like they were old friends almost immediately, both relieved they had found an ally so readily in their new surroundings. Seeing Elizabeth in the distance chatting to a group of girls, Josh was transfixed.

"My God!" Josh said. "She is beautiful."

"Who?" Zach asked.

"Over there, in the floral dress with her hair tied back. The tall blonde."

"Her? Really?"

"What are you thinking! Of course her! She is absolutely gorgeous! I have to meet her..."

Zach laughed. "I'm sure you'll get your chance, we're only just starting. We're all stuck here for the next few years."

Josh couldn't keep from staring. She had such a relaxed way about her. Smiling effortlessly, she seemed to intoxicate those around her with her warmth. She turned towards Josh and waved.

He couldn't believe it. He slowly started to speak, "Zach, she's...waving...at... me!"

Zach laughed again, "Well, wave back, you don't want to be rude!"

He felt so stupid, but he stood there with a dumbstruck smile on his face and waved with Zach. Josh managed a stilted motion with his hand that Zach mimicked, the two waving in unison. Elizabeth started laughing hysterically and ran over towards them.

"Oh my God, she's coming over! Shit, shit, shit!"

"Relax man, take it easy!" Zach laughed.

"So who's the fellow comedian?" she asked Zach, still giggling.

"Elizabeth, this is Josh."

Even more beautiful in person, Elizabeth stood at five foot nine, had long blonde hair, big green eyes and small freckles across her petite nose. Full red lips, with a tanned complexion and wearing no makeup, she looked like the stereotypical Aussie beach girl, but with such kindness beaming from her stunning smile. Josh was in love.

He extended his hand. "A pleasure to meet you, Elizabeth."

"Thanks. Nice to meet you, too."

Now totally lost for words, Josh asked the obvious. "So, how do you two know each other?"

"Really? Can't you tell?" Elizabeth answered. "This is my baby brother!" She reached over and messed up his hair.

"Hey, take it easy! I'm a total of three minutes younger than her."

"You're twins?" Josh asked in disbelief, with Zach nodding his head in acknowledgement.

"Yeah, well I'm still your elder, mister, and don't you forget it!" she giggled. "So when you guys are done here we should go for lunch. They must have some good vegetarian food around here *surely*."

With that meeting, the paths of the next four years of their lives became intertwined. Elizabeth had fallen for Josh not long after meeting him, but managed to draw their courtship out over the next couple of months, both savoring the experience. The three of them were soon inseparable, and Josh had never been so happy. Josh had never had a friend like Zach, with both of them enjoying a profound connection. With Zach he was able to talk about things that had floated around in his consciousness for as long as he could remember, but had always felt too strange to express.

After his sheltered upbringing in a small country town, Josh was now surrounded by new exciting ideas and experiences that fundamentally shifted his worldview.

The Holtzman twins both seemed wise beyond their years and he felt lucky to have been welcomed into their special club.

Elizabeth was simply the kindest person he had ever met. Always pursuing some righteous cause, she seemed to see and feel all the suffering of the world and was determined to make a difference. She had a legion of followers ready to assist her, with every act performed geared toward the goal of serving others. This was especially so with Josh, whom she loved with all her heart. She felt gifted that she was given the chance to help open Josh up to the world around him and witness the wonderment that this often brought. Together, they got to explore romantic love for the first time, with their feelings only deepening as time passed. They were both convinced that they had found their life partner. However, they never discussed this as it seemed like such an obvious truth that didn't need to be raised.

Unfortunately for both of them, their unspoken wish would never transpire.

It all started as they approached their final exams in their fourth year. Elizabeth began to complain about a pain in her right side just beneath her rib cage. She had been to her doctor a couple of times, but they were unable to find a problem. Elizabeth figured she had bumped herself during one of her many adventures and tried to put it out of her mind.

The pain eased somewhat over the next few weeks, but it was still there and became a constant source of worry for Josh in particular. He felt an inexplicable sense of unease surrounding the localized pain. Continuing to insist that she should go see another doctor, Elisabeth finally relented when the pain worsened again. Still finding nothing immediately wrong but aware of their concern, the doctor proceeded to run a full gamut of tests to try and isolate the problem.

This added diligence proved justified, but in finding a diagnosis, three young lives were destroyed.

Elizabeth was diagnosed with Hepatocellular Carcinoma, a primary cancer of the liver. It was extremely rare in western countries, especially in cases where a history of hepatitis was not present. This explained the difficulty in diagnosis. It was just not something one would look for in a healthy twenty-one year old Australian woman. The most crushing thing about this particular disease was its prognosis. On average, the five year survival rate for those diagnosed with this cancer was less than five per cent, with most patients dying in three to six months of their initial diagnosis.

In an effort to support Elizabeth and Zach, Josh assumed the role of the stoic optimist.

Relentless in his positivity, he refused to acknowledge the terminal nature of her situation, finding numerous examples of cases where patients had beat the odds in a vain attempt to prove that all was not lost.

Due to the advanced nature of her cancer, the only possibility of prolonging her life was radical surgery which was undertaken only days after the definitive diagnosis. Compounding the already hopeless situation, at best, the surgery could only remove a small part of the large tumor mass due to is precarious location nestled around her hepatic artery. This failure ensured that Elizabeth would not survive for much longer. In the end it was just forty-three more days.

Elizabeth accepted her fate graciously and with her selfless nature was most concerned with how Josh and her brother would cope with her loss. With Josh's mask firmly in place, he assured her that he would manage, even though he knew that this was completely untrue. The last image he held of his first love was after her death, letting go of her hand that he had been holding for her final four hours.

Josh was devastated by her passing. The memory of her corpse tainted all his living memories of Elizabeth, with every mental excursion he made to a time when she was alive infected by images of her pale, lifeless body.

With tears again flowing freely from thoughts of his profound loss, Josh's attention gradually shifted back to his immediate surroundings. Still lying on his couch in front of his TV, an ice cream commercial was playing. It depicted a happy couple playfully feeding each other pieces of falling chocolate from their respective treats.

Josh stared blankly at the dancing imagery for a moment until it was replaced by a commercial advertising a mortician's funeral services. Josh was suddenly hit with a stark realization…"I NEED ICE CREAM!"

He made his way down to a nearby convenience store, picking up his ice cream and some essential items necessary after his period of solitary confinement. He rang Kush as he shopped to seek some support and relay some of the weird coincidences that he had been experiencing during his extended TV odyssey.   His friend was eager to write these events off as mere chance, and was further convinced that Josh was 'losing his mind'. Kush quickly ended the conversation when he realized that he would not be able to get any 'sense' out of Josh yet again. At this point, Josh was at the checkout, mindlessly handing over the items from his shopping basket.

After overhearing part of the telephone conversation, the sales assistant began to speak.

"Sounds like a synchronicity…" she commented as she continued to scan his items.

"Sorry… a what?" Josh asked.

"I'm sorry, I couldn't help overhearing. Ummm. What you were talking about. It sounds like a synchronicity!"

"I'm sorry, but I don't know what that means." Josh replied, slightly embarrassed.

"I think of it as a 'meaningful coincidence'. I seem to have them all the time. They really make me feel as if I'm part of something greater than myself, that no matter what happens, it will all work out." She blushed, and looked down, continuing to speak. "I know that sounds kind of silly saying that out loud … but you shouldn't ignore them. I find they usually happen, or I notice them happening, when I really need to find something…"

"Like what?"

"I don't know, I'm never sure. The next path I need to take…in life?" she laughed. "That'll be $15.65."

Josh thanked and paid the cashier and made his way back out onto the street, pondering what he had been told.

"A meaningful coincidence. It seems like a contradiction in terms.

A coincidence is by definition not meaningful, merely the product of chance. But there does seem to be something to what she was saying and what I am experiencing," he thought.

He hurried home to scour his dictionary.

> *Synchronicity – The simultaneous occurrence of events which appear meaningfully related but have no discoverable causal connection. See C.G. Jung.*

As he finished reading the definition, four distinctive bells chimed from his phone notifying him of a text from Kush.

> *I'm worried about you man. I hate to say it, but you are a different person since the accident, and I'm not sure I like who you are becoming. I mean, fuck, get real man! These questions that you're asking me, you really seem like you're fucking losing it! Pull yourself together. When you do, give me a call, we can bed some chicks and you can forget any of this shit ever happened!*

He dropped his phone. Josh had been aware of Kush's ambivalence toward his new found enquiries, but he never thought he would be totally abandoned by him.

He was once again overcome with feelings of isolation. Kush had no concept of the fact that Josh would have loved to have gone back to the person he was before. Life was so simple. Focusing purely on the superficialities of existence leaves little time to ponder anything of depth. If one did find such time, such thoughts would only have the potential to lead to significant states of mental malaise that Josh was now only too aware of.

He collapsed onto his couch and let his head rest to the side. His eyes fell on an open magazine on the floor. It was an article on Albert Einstein that he had been distracting himself with earlier, but all he could see now was a single, highlighted quote:

> *Great spirits have always encountered violent opposition from mediocre minds.*

Another synchronicity. The truth of this phrase from beyond the grave of the former intellectual giant resonated through him. It provided some solace to think that it may not be him who is lost, but those bemused souls from his former life.

He realized he could no longer sit alone in his apartment, wallowing in self-pity. He must take action, but what course of action was available to him? It was clear that his workplace was of no comfort, merely amplifying any feelings of alienation and loss he was experiencing. His friends were either openly abandoning him due to his newly inherited perspective, or grossly ill equipped to offer the metaphysical or existential advice he now craved. Thoughts of Elizabeth and the happiness he once enjoyed continued to arise. He knew that she would have been able to support him on the path of spiritual and philosophical inquiry that he was now being led down, an able partner and friend on a journey fraught with the potential for psychic harm.

But, of course such deliberations were futile. No partnership was to be enjoyed, no help provided by those that have long left this earth. It was at this point that the answer to his dilemma became plainly obvious.

Zach.

He needed to find Zach. Although they had not spoken since Elizabeth's funeral, Zach was the only person who Josh trusted that may be of help to him at this time. From memory, Zach had fervently pursued a similar line of inner inquiry while finishing his degree, with this only intensifying after his sister's death. He desperately hoped that his old friend would be able to help guide him through his current state of psychological turmoil. Josh smiled, feeling a genuine sense of optimism for the first time since his accident, his way forward now crystallized before him.

chapter 3

Josh's indicator blinked on his M powered 5 series BMW as he made the left turn into the entrance of his old university. After careful consideration he knew that this was the place his search must begin. Having travelled back to Zach's hometown to find his mother, he was met with sad news that she had died of a stroke five years earlier. As Zach's father had died when he was a child, this left no family that Josh knew of.

Although he had continued to probe, any further inquiries into the whereabouts of Zach in his hometown proved fruitless. This forced him to reflect on who was close to Zach when they were still friends. One person immediately came to mind: Zach's favorite philosophy lecturer, Lloyd Woodford. Zach had felt an immediate connection to Lloyd in his early university days. Indeed, it was Lloyd's genius that inspired Zach to pursue a major in Philosophy.

In the latter years of their degree, he would often find the pair in the philosopher's lounge embroiled in intense debate on one philosophical issue or another. It was with Lloyd that he knew he should be able to find some clue to Zach's whereabouts.

Travelling down the meandering entrance road to the university was a surprisingly uncomfortable experience for Josh. He felt like he was disturbing the ghost of his past self by entering this domain, something that he had not considered may be a traumatic experience. Everywhere he looked he was reminded of his former idealism, held up as a mirror here to reveal his distorted self that existed today. However, any angst caused by walking the hallowed grounds of his former life was a minor cost to find Zach. The question of his own whereabouts for the past 10 years was a deeper issue, not yet ready to be probed.

The university grounds were obviously familiar to him but as he had not explored them since his final exam, a lot had changed.

After Elizabeth's death and his subsequent falling out with Zach, he didn't even attend his graduation ceremony, preferring the anonymity of his graduation certificate arriving in the mail.

The existing architecture had now been encroached upon by a variety of later structures, with glass, concrete and metal abounding. Manicured gardens and select water features had also been added to the landscape, no doubt to curry favor with perspective international students and their international dollars. Such features that fit well on the cover of a student prospectus were seen as a wise business decision, much more so than retaining knowledgeable Humanities professors.

After parking his car in the visitor's car park, he proceeded to the Arts precinct.

The Arts and Humanities building was a rectangular monolith, 13 stories of concrete that dominated the landscape of the university to this day. Upon entry, it did not appear that much had been done in terms of refurbishment, other than the addition of a cafe on the foyer level and a new glass entry structure linking the outer world with within. With the perpetual underfunding of the Arts and Humanities departments over the years, this was hardly a surprise. In an increasingly privatized world, one stood to lose everything if one couldn't easily demonstrate value in the only currency that seemed to matter: money. Proficiency in ethereal disciplines such as critical analysis and a heightened historical and cultural awareness didn't quite compute in dollars and cents, but yet impacted society positively in countless ways. However when faced with competition for funding from IT and engineering in a cash starved university, the battle was over before any sword was drawn. Josh remembered protesting for ideals such as these but now had the feeling their voices had little effect.

Josh walked across the foyer and proceeded to navigate the narrow escalators that penetrated the middle of the building, travelling on what was affectionately known during his student days as 'the cattle run'. Upon arriving on the 9th floor, he walked into the Philosophy department to locate Lloyd's office. As it was mid-way through the semester, the floor was filled with students.

He checked in with the reception and located Lloyd in room 923. He knocked and waited.

He was greeted by an educated British accent.

"Yes? The door is open."

He opened the door to find a small, cramped office.

Its walls were lined with bookcases, all overflowing with books. There were two red felt covered padded chairs in the center of the room and a desk supporting an aging computer sitting idle towards the back. A small window permitted the only natural light and a view to the surrounding university grounds.

Lloyd had his eyes focused on a student essay with his red pen poised in the air for the next comment. Without looking up he asked, "How can I help you?"

Lloyd Woodford was a thin man in his mid-fifty's. Standing at five foot nine, he had a learned face, thinning black hair and brown eyes, viewing the world through a pair of horn rimmed glasses. He was wearing a worn brown jacket, brown slacks and a lime green shirt with matching lime green socks.

"I was wondering if you could help me." Josh started. "I'm trying to track down an old friend. I believe he was a student of yours, Zach Holtzman?"

Lloyd's eyes remained fixated on the sheet before him as he finished a lengthy annotation. Josh began to move his feet nervously as he stood waiting in silence for a response. With a final stroke of his pen, Lloyd reached over for its lid and efficiently replaced it. Placing the paper on the top of a nearby pile of essays, he looked up at Josh for the first time, pushing his glasses with his finger towards the bridge of his nose.

"Mr. Holtzman. Zach. Yes! An extremely bright lad. His sister's death was a terrible tragedy. And whom may I ask would like to know?"

"My name is Josh. Josh Black. I am an old friend of Zach's from University." Josh replied.

"Josh? Hmmmm..." He rested his elbows on the arms of his chair. Opening his hands in front of him, his fingertips met as he thumbed through the files of his mind.

"I think I remember him mentioning you. From my last meeting with Zach it seemed that you left your friend quite distraught at a very difficult time for him."

"It was a difficult time for us all." Josh responded defensively.

"I spoke to him not long after the funeral. He was understandably distressed but I believe this was exacerbated by a conversation that he had with you?"

"You have a good memory. Unfortunately, that was the last conversation I had with him." replied Josh.

"I seem to recall that he was extremely upset about a comment made by the priest after the funeral. Something about taking comfort in the fact that 'this was all part of God's plan...'"

"A tired cliché. I vaguely remember him mentioning that."

"Zach had a very sharp analytical mind, which over his degree was highly tuned to philosophical inquiry." Lloyd stood up out of his chair and began walking across the room.

"Under normal circumstances I'm sure that he'd have taken the priest to task immediately for such a comment. Instead, given it was his sister's funeral, he didn't want anything to take away from that. So he bit his tongue and let the comment stew."

Josh's eyes fell towards the ground as he was filled with guilt.

"I believe he tried to talk to you about this?"

"I think he did..."

Lloyd took the vacant seat across from Josh, motioning for him to sit down. "Yes. But finding no consolation from you, he became consumed by a dystopian vision of reality."

Lloyd clasped his hands in front of him and lent towards Josh. "One where fatalism was king..."

"Fatalism?" Josh asked.

"Yes. The doctrine where all choice, all free action is merely an illusion. Where the future is wholly pre-determined and there is not a thing that anyone can do about it."

"But that sounds like the opposite of what Zach believed. He was always one to encourage people to act on what they believed in... to try and make a difference in the world in which they lived."

"That doesn't surprise me. Notions of fatalism, free will and determinism are often discussed within philosophy classrooms. These were topics I believe he had quite a passion for. I think it was part of the reason why I took to Zach as a student. I could relate to his enthusiastic attempts to elucidate a clear argument in favor of free will..."

"But Professor, hang on. This whole notion of fate... isn't it just ridiculous? Just something someone believes when they can't claim ownership of the decisions that they've made in their lives? Of course we are free to choose what we do. It's just that many of us may regret the choices that we've made."

A wry smile crept over Lloyd's face. "Really? Well, philosophers throughout the ages haven't been so sure Josh, and for good reason."

Lloyd suddenly clapped his hands together with the loud noise filling the room. Josh was startled, jumping in his seat and instinctively grabbing its wooden arm rests.

"So you don't believe in fatalism?" Lloyd asked. "Well, to be honest it's quite an extreme position that is not supported by many. But do you believe in science?"

Josh hesitated, sensing he was being led into a trap.

"Sure. Although I don't think the question makes sense. Knowledge that science provides us is obviously true. Just look at the world around us. The modern world was created by science."

"Very true. But that doesn't mean that science has told us anything real about the universe. It only means that it has given us the tools to manipulate our world for certain gain and often unintended loss. But I digress. So do you believe that there are certain universal laws that govern our universe?"

"Yes!" Josh stated affirmatively.

"And those laws are subject to everything within the universe?"

He hesitated slightly "...Yes."

"So how does your concept of 'free will' fit into such a universe if all is governed by universal law? How does that leave room for choice?"

"To be honest, I hadn't really thought about it before. So what you are trying to say is that if we are free we must be violating the laws of the universe?"

"No, no, no. You missed my point. I'm merely trying to illustrate that the question is not as simple as it may first appear."

Lloyd again rose from his chair.

"Cause and effect. You have one particular set of circumstances that entail another." He extended his palms out to his sides.

"I go to clap my hands..." he quickly brought his palms towards each other, stopping just short of touching, "...and you flinch in anticipation of the sound."

Josh felt embarrassed as he had indeed flinched again. He could feel his cheeks turn red as they filled with blood. Smiling, Lloyd sat back down and continued.

"We see the principle of cause and effect at work every day of our lives. Indeed, it is how we predict future events. If I see a car driving at great speed towards a brick wall and I have previously drained that particular car of brake fluid, I think it's reasonable to say that it will crash into that wall. The cause, me draining the brake fluid. The effect, the car crashing into the wall."

"So what? What's this got to do with anything?"

"One may hold that *we*, human beings, are all bound by universal laws. Say we include the law of causation. Then one could argue that each and every one of us is causally determined to make the choices that we do throughout our lives. So I have a decision in the morning to have toast or cereal. Now to me, I seem to wake up and *choose* what breakfast I will have. But in reality, it is the sum total of all the previous experience that I have had that causally propels me to make the choice of bread over Cheerios."

"Isn't this just like what we were talking about before? Fatalism?"

"Some would argue yes. But strictly speaking we are now talking about a form of causal determinism. Some people believe that you can be still free even if you are causally determined in all of your decisions in life."

"What? Now you've lost me."

"Compatibilists contend that as long as you are not forcibly coerced by someone or something in your choice, you have made it freely, despite being causally compelled to do so. Some variant of this position is what is commonly held in the philosophical community today. I personally believe this is so, simply for its philosophical salience. It is much easier to make sense of the world in this way. You don't give up free will, and you haven't bestowed upon sentient beings a mysterious power, beyond the laws of science, to shape reality as they see fit.

This problem is somewhat altered today thanks to modern physics and quantum mechanics which seems to illustrate a fundamentally indeteriminisitic view of reality.

Instead of A causing B, you have a case where A has a ninety five percent chance of leading to B, or a five percent chance of leading to C. Try as some might, however, this does not leave room for free will. Cause has been simply replaced with random chance. But again, I digress."

Lloyd picked up his capped red pen and began twirling it between his index finger and thumb, continuing to speak.

"Now our friend Zach's problem wasn't so much one of causal determinism. Indeed not one of determinism of any kind. It was more one of the conferred power and foresight of God."

"But Zach wasn't particularly religious. At least he wasn't back then…" Josh stated.

"In confronting death and facing mortality so intimately, questions of God and religion are very common." Lloyd said.

Josh thought back wondering if he had any such considerations at that time. All he could remember was the anger and pain he felt when Elizabeth was taken from him and his unspoken vow never to allow himself to be hurt like that again. His vow was kept as promised, but at massive costs that he could never have foreseen.

"There are some commonly held assumptions concerning the abilities that God possesses in most major monotheistic religions of today. For starters, God is said to be omnipotent, meaning God is all powerful. He can do anything. Thus, if God wanted to, he could control our every action. He could also make us believe that we were free to choose what we did, even though He was the one making the decisions. Thus, our freedom is contingent on the whim of God. At any time, our tenuous freedom could be removed."

Josh nodded his head in understanding.

"God is also said to be omniscient, God knows everything. He knows all past events and knows everything that will happen in the future. You can see the problem that this presents to freedom. If there is a set body of knowledge about the future, how could we choose something other than how God knows we will act?"

"So in the end, how can God exist and we be free?" Josh asked.

"An excellent question. Well, there are two obvious possibilities. You could adjust your conception of our freedom – for example, the compatibilist, who believes in the simultaneous truth of causal determinism and free will wouldn't have these problems. The other option is to adjust your view of God..."

"By changing the powers that we ascribe him?"

"Exactly." Lloyd answered, nodding his head.

"To be perfectly frank, I have no idea how to handle such a dilemma. What did Zach make of this?" Josh asked.

"Zach took a step back from the problem itself and started questioning the whole idea of needing 'to know' something."

"I'm not sure what you mean?" Josh questioned.

"There is a whole field of philosophy called epistemology devoted to questions of knowledge, with none more fundamental than 'What does it mean to know something?' We all go on thinking that it's plainly obvious that we know all kinds of things about the world."

"Well...Yeah, of course we do!"

"Yes, but like so many things that we accept unquestionably, as soon as you push a little deeper, things are not quite so self-evident. Anyway, that's beside the point. After speaking to the priest, Zach was profoundly upset as you know. He went away and made a list of all the possible retorts he could make to the priest but ended up being less convinced of what he *knew* before he started!"

Lloyd glanced up at the clock on his wall, lent over his desk and picked up some books.

"Come. I have class in 10 minutes. Walk with me."

Josh nodded and stood up, holding the door open for the professor and following close behind him, still listening intently.

With students passing by left and right as they walked, Lloyd continued.

"Zach realized that his arguments were certainly more compelling than what the priest had said, and he had numerous retorts for any number of possible counter arguments that the priest may have made.

But, despite all this knowledge, he couldn't find any truly compelling reason why one would believe what he did. Why he was *right* in believing that we are free."

"Surely if he had the more compelling argument that is enough to say he is right?"

"Sure, as a philosopher that is exactly why one person would be believed over another. But this wasn't about belief. His beliefs were probably more well-grounded than the priest's in reasoned argument but that didn't bring him any closer to knowing if he was right. He realized that he could never *know* if he was free, if anyone was truly free..."

They pushed open the glass doors, exiting the department and proceeding down the escalators. The hum of student chatter surrounded them as they walked.

"Why did this affect him so much?"

"He had just been told that his sister's death was part of God's plan. In his mind this was equivalent to saying that we are all merely actors on a stage. Elizabeth's death, and indeed every single act in our lives, were all just whims dictated by God. Remove God from the equation and insert causality, or quantum indeterminism and we are all still puppets mesmerized by the illusion of freedom.

As humans, we all live our lives with a common belief that we have free will, that we are free to make the choices that are presented to us throughout our lives. So much follows from this. We can discuss all the ways which our free will can be impinged upon or taken away, like through manipulation by external forces, such as our parents, our peers, or on a larger scale, the media or our governments. We even go to war and kill our fellow human beings in the name of freedom! But there is a question beyond all this: Are we really ever free to choose anything?"

They both rounded the end of one escalator and proceeded down the next one travelling to the floor below. Lloyd continued his point... "If we are not free, then our whole society, our entire system of rules and laws must be thrown out. A foundational premise in our world is that, if not coerced, forced, or mentally incapable we are always free to choose what we do. Thus, the life that we have is our own making. If we are rich and happy, it is through beneficial choices that we made, if we are a criminal that has been incarcerated, we are only caged due to our own freely made decisions.

If there is no choice there can be no responsibility. To determine whether someone is worthy of congratulations or derision is premised on the idea that they were free to choose what they did. This is like what you said before about claiming ownership over the choices one has made in their lives. What you were talking about was taking responsibility for those choices. Without freedom, there can be no responsibility. We do not congratulate the white billiard ball that knocks the black into the corner pocket, as we don't lock up the bullet that penetrates a man's skull. We believe there are free agents behind the movement of both objects, *responsible* for the movement of both objects."

"I can appreciate all that, and now understand Zach's conundrum: How can we *know* if we are truly free or not?"

"Exactly! Well, with philosophy you can't. There is no argument that one could make that could deductively prove that we are free. We can't provide a definitive proof either way from the perspective of science either.

Although as it stands now, the evidence is certainly leaning towards an indeterministic universe in my opinion."

"Well that's useless..." Josh said, "What's the point of philosophy then?"

"I think philosophy's main strength lies in the tools it provides to help critically analyze one's beliefs, so that one may make an informed judgment of what they believe and why they believe it. So many people hold beliefs that are in blatant contradiction to others that they may hold, with these inconsistencies permeating throughout their lives. Through philosophy one can gradually purge oneself of such inconsistencies, changing ones beliefs in the process to be more in line with one's perception of the world. But in the end, all beliefs, all arguments, come to rest on a set of assumed premises. You can have the most logically consistent argument in the world, but if you don't agree with the premises or assumptions behind it, you cannot accept it."

They left the humanities building and turned toward the nearby lecture theatre. The campus was bustling with activity, with students and teachers everywhere darting between classes.

Lloyd continued, "I could appreciate his difficulty, but I am at peace with these facts. I know that there are many things that I believe that I can never truly know for sure, but I have accepted this."

"And Zach?" Josh asked.

"No, I'm afraid that this was totally unacceptable to him. For his sister, a truly benevolent soul of this world to be indiscriminately taken as she was, well before her time, reeked of a fundamental injustice. Zach had men of God talking to him about the unseen wisdom of the Creator, but this whole idea of having 'faith' in the Supreme Being that they themselves held responsible for this atrocity seemed to him to be ludicrous."

They arrived at the lecture theatre and stopped at the door. "I had a friend from a science background that experienced a similar crisis in his beliefs. He was born and bred a scientist, but he came to a point in his life where he lost his fundamental faith in his discipline. He set out on an alternative path of discovery, shifting his focus from the external world that we are obsessed with in our modern age, to the world we all find within. I introduced Zach to him for this very reason."

"So would he know where Zach is?" Josh asked.

"Maybe. I did send Zach off to visit him and I haven't heard from him since.

So that would be where I would start."

He lent down on one of his books and scribbled on a piece of paper.

"Here are his details. Say hello from me if you visit him. I haven't seen William in years."

"Thank you, Lloyd, for your help."

"You're welcome Josh. I hope you find what you are looking for."

He shook Josh's hand and quickly disappeared amongst the sea of students pouring into his lecture.

chapter 4

Josh rounded the bend to more natural beauty. He had spent the previous two hours navigating the southern Victorian coastline along the Great Ocean Road. Following along the meandering path, he was witness to sheer cliffs, nestled beach communities, clusters of trees and pockets of farmland. A bitter wind rolled off Bass Strait, carrying air from the Southern Ocean and the Antarctic continent, further cooling the land on what was already a cold winter day. The unsettled sea thrashed against the exposed limestone walls, continuing the ancient erosion process from eons past. Low lying clouds were beginning to disperse, allowing some diffuse rays of sunlight access to the turbulent blue ocean.

Just before reaching the township of Apollo Bay, Josh turned inland away from the coastal road. Maneuvering along winding roads and steep inclines, he arrived at a country that was both beautiful and expansive. From the zenith of the hill he had just climbed the vista stretched for miles in every direction, punctuated by large clusters of trees, rocks and various agricultural enterprises.

The evening sun sat large on the horizon, about to depart for the day with the first stars already present to take its place. Josh had only visited the bush a few times throughout his life, urban bound for no other reason than not realizing there was an alternative. As he appreciated his surroundings, he wondered why this was so.

Doctor Oberson lived on a farm with an eclectic mix of animals and plants. As Josh entered the property, he was greeted by horses, goats and a couple of kangaroos, all peering curiously at him through a wire fence. To his left, a number of fruit trees were aligned symmetrically, with some deep red apples appearing ready for harvest. Free range chickens strutted around their large pen, stretching their wings and feeding from the ground, living their lives unaware of the miserable alternatives lived by billions of their species.

He could make out a large greenhouse in the distance and numerous expansive vegetable gardens.

A collection of photovoltaic solar cells were present on the roof of the main house, capturing the last few photons offered by the sun for the day.

Josh parked his car at the front of the house. The slightly unkempt facade fit effortlessly into its surroundings. Long tufts of grass appeared near its corners, with exposed wood panels and large blocks of bluestone forming its walls and dark green corrugated iron providing the roof. The collection of carefully chosen materials gave the impression that the house had indeed risen from the ground, like it was simply another feature of the surrounding natural landscape.

He walked around the side of the house and could see a towering figure in the distance. A large hammer in one hand and a long cylindrical post in the other, the man was walking slowly, arranging the pieces of a puzzle he was creating. Josh leapt over a nearby fence and walked across a large paddock.

Approaching from behind, Josh called out, "Are you Doctor Oberson?"

Hunched over a collection of thick fence posts, the figure expelled a subdued laugh.

"I haven't been referred to in that way for a while," he said as he turned around, releasing the wooden post he held with a gentle thud. "Call me Will."

William Oberson was a massive man. Standing at over six foot seven with a barrel chest and thick broad shoulders, he looked to be more at home felling giant trees in a forest than sporting a white coat in a laboratory. He slouched selfconsciously when standing, with his rounded shoulders slightly diminishing his gargantuan stature.

"And what can I do for you, Mister...?"

"Black. Josh Black."

They shook hands as Josh told Will what had brought him there.

"So how is Lloyd?" Will asked. "I do miss our chats, but one of the consequences of my life here is that I seldom get out."

"He seems well and sends his regards." Josh replied. "So, do you remember Zach?"

"Of course I do! My memory hasn't quite failed me yet young man!" he boomed back with an added chuckle.

He picked up the post he was previously carrying and carefully placed the tapered end in a freshly dug hole.

"From what I remember of your friend, he was a particularly driven fellow and quite disillusioned. So given the history of my falling out with the scientific establishment, I quickly grew to like him."

Will picked up the sledgehammer that he previously held and returned to the post.

He turned his head and looked back at Josh. "I hope I was able to stimulate some thought and help him on his quest…"

Loosening his shoulders and bending his knees, he unleashed the sledge. Swinging it in a wide arc above him, the heavy metal head came to land precisely on top of the post, driving it into the ground. Will repeated the action a few times until the post had reached the depth he desired. Josh recoiled slightly each time the hammer struck, his face again flushed with embarrassment.

"You okay?" Will asked.

"I'm fine." Josh answered, his crimson face only deepening in color with the added attention. Quickly focusing again on what had brought him there, Josh asked, "Do you think Zach knew what he was doing?"

Will dropped the sledgehammer again and looked back at Josh with a wide grin.

"What an interesting question! What exactly are you talking about – him knowing what he was doing? Do *you* know what you are doing? Does *anyone* know what they are doing? Or more importantly, *why* they are doing what they do?"

"What are *you* talking about?" Josh exclaimed, his head spinning from the retort.

Will stood up straight and dusted off his hands.

"Zach was more aware than most people. He was asking some of the few fundamental questions that have plagued mankind since we had the vocabulary to express them! The questions rarely change, but the people that ask them come and go throughout the ages."

"Isn't that why he came to you? Because you're a scientist? So you had answers for him?" Josh asked in an insistent jumble of words.

"A scientist!" Will laughed. "Another thing I haven't been called in a long while. So you think a scientist has answers to these questions, do you? Well I guess scientists are cast as the priests of our age, the seers and givers of wisdom... and of course technology..."

"So you didn't have answers for him then?" Josh asked.

"Josh, I could sympathize with the questions that Zach had and merely shared with him paths that I had travelled on my own search. My training as a scientist in all this was a blessing and a curse."

The sun was beginning to dip below the horizon, coloring the distant clouds in a vibrant red.

"I find that hard to believe." Josh stated. "Your scientific objectivity should equip you better than most to find answers if you were any kind of scientist!"

"Objectivity? Ha!" he shouted, shaking his head. "One of the great modern myths, the pure objectivity of science." He picked up another long post from his pile, walking over to the next hole in the sequence.

"Can you grab the sledge and bring it over here?" Will asked.

Josh struggled as he picked up the heavy tool. After Will's effortless application, he had completely misjudged its weight.

"How can you say that?" Josh groaned. "Evidence for the truth of science is in everything we see and do in our lives... and you're a scientist. I would have thought you would need the least convincing of anyone!" Shuffling along the ground, Josh strained as he placed the sledge in Will's hands.

"WAS a scientist, Josh. Now I would prefer to define myself as a child mystic, aware of the myriad of possibilities that surround me but only just now learning to open my eyes."

"But..." Josh tried to interject as Will cut him off.

"Josh, because of the inherently human endeavor that is science, how could one honestly hope for any real objectivity?"

Will pounded the fence post into the ground with three quick strokes.

"But I thought we had methods, procedures in place to negate our subjective, emotional tendencies?" Josh asked.

"We do, indeed. But the methods and procedures you refer to are part of the problem my boy. We follow the scientific method; valuing observable, repeatable, empirical results above all else. What is considered observable, what one holds to be real empirical data, is all influenced by the paradigm of the day. I guess part of the problem I see is that one is trained in the dogmatic acceptance of this paradigm as a young scientist. Thus, one then is much more likely to not see anything that would challenge this. Indeed, one will instinctively argue to defend the method against any detractors. This is especially so in the case of the 'Gold standard' in pharmaceutical studies – 'the double blind placebo controlled trial'."

"So you are alone in seeing these shortcomings?"

"Not at all. I think many working scientists have at the very least twinges of insight into this. But most dismiss these thoughts without any real consideration, as any such subversion challenges the very foundations of the very careers that they have built!"

"Okay then, that may be all true but it still doesn't refute what I said. With all the technology that we have and the world that we've built from scientific progress, doesn't this validate what we're doing beyond anything else?"

"Really?" Will asked. "Climate change, mass species extinction, simultaneous famines and obesity epidemics, modern warfare – all are heavily influenced by our advancement of science. I don't know if one could credibly argue that they demonstrate how advanced we are."

"Fair enough. But I think you know what I was getting at." Josh replied.

"Okay, but I hope you take my point. Yes, I will agree that modern science is technically skilled at making up rules that give us a degree of control over our surrounding world, for good or bad. But as far as science having illuminated definitive, fundamental truths about the universe and our place in it, I am yet to be convinced."

Will leaned on the newly planted post, testing its stability.

"I'm not sure what you mean?" Josh enquired.

"Instrumentalism is the view that holds science is excellent at being used as an instrument to make calculations, predictions and build things, but doesn't make any claims that the laws are a description of how things actually are. Basically, reducing science to the role of a convenient calculation tool."

"Come on," Josh said skeptically. "Surely there are loads of things that we know to be true..."

"Of course, there were so many things that we just *knew* to be true. Like we *knew* that the Sun orbited the earth. Isn't it obvious! We see it rise up every morning, move overhead and set at night. We *knew* for almost two thousand years that draining blood from a person would cure them of a whole range of illnesses! We *knew* that the chemical DDT was an extremely safe pesticide. We *knew* thalidomide was a safe, effective treatment for morning sickness..."

"I know what you're getting at," interjected Josh. "We've been wrong before so why won't we continue to be proven wrong in the future?"

"I think that's an obvious truth. But there are other reasons to question the objectivity of the whole scientific enterprise."

"Such as?"

"Well, I think most people unconsciously subscribe to the view that science is forever edging closer and closer to some grand truth, building piece by piece on the knowledge and experience of our forefathers."

Josh's mind drifted back to a documentary he had seen during his recent television marathon.

"You mean like... what's it called? The GUT?"

"Yes, exactly! The holy grail of modern physics, the Grand Unified Theory. Aiming to unify all of the fundamental forces known to man. Well, a man by the name of Thomas Kuhn thought of things a little differently. In the early 60's his book, 'The Structure of Scientific Revolutions', directly challenged the prevailing ideology, with its influence spreading from the realms of science and philosophy to the social sciences."

Will tossed the mighty hammer over his shoulder, resting it there. He then knelt over and picked up his nearby toolbox from the moist turf at their feet.

"Come. I'm done here for the day. Would you care to join me for some tea?"

Josh, still trying to digest what had been discussed, welcomed the respite. "Thanks. Much appreciated."

They walked through the paddock along the long line of empty holes that Will was yet to fill. At the end of the cleared grassland a stone path revealed itself, beckoning them inside a lush temperate rainforest. The dense canopy of trees and the day's late hour ensured that their walk would be obscured through dim light. Surrounding trunks and branches easily hid native residents, their existence only betrayed by their voices signaling the end of the day. Josh followed closely behind Will as they walked silently down the path. He was disappointed that he had arrived at dusk as he could sense he was missing a wonderful journey. The various silhouettes surrounding him hid an abundant natural beauty only now available to him through his nose. Fragrant smells emanating from the nearby ferns, Myrtle Beech and Eucalyptus trees mixed with the moist cool air into an intoxicating natural cocktail. Josh breathed deeply, savoring the fresh air.

After their short walk they arrived at a clearing near the main residence. Will walked to a nearby shed where he placed his tools inside the steel door and shut it behind him. He then led Josh to a neatly paved section located at the rear of his house. A solid oak table occupied the center of the area, with a partially covered outdoor kitchen located to one side. Will fired one of the gas burners on the barbeque and filled a well-worn kettle with water from a nearby tap, placing it on top.

"Please take a seat" Will offered with an outstretched hand. Josh took a place at the table, sitting on one of the dark wooden chairs.

"Now, where were we?" Will asked, leaning on a nearby bench.

"You mentioned Thomas..."

"...Kuhn! That's right. Kuhn's book challenged the idea that science progressed in incremental steps. The commonly held belief was that science was a historically cumulative endeavor, with each generation's discoveries providing the foundations for those that followed them, and so on and so on. Each new scientific discovery was added to the vast storehouse of knowledge. This provided the possibility of the next scientist adding the next piece of the puzzle with the whole process slowly edging closer to the 'truth'."

Will produced some fragrant herbs from a glass jar beneath the stove. Sprinkling some in an ornate teapot, he continued to speak.

"Kuhn did not argue against this occurring. Rather, he held that such periods of 'normal science' were the main work of scientists, solving problems and answering questions that followed from the paradigm of the day. Such work, however, was not where science displayed its real moments of change. This only happened when the current framework of thought was transformed in its entirety, with the paradigm of the day replaced with another through the process of revolution."

"What do you mean by paradigm?" Josh asked.

"A Kuhnian paradigm is the semantic framework through which one views the world. It is the complete set of assumptions and labels that one carries to 'make sense' of what they see. This is why such revolutions are so traumatic for those involved. This is especially so for those greatly bonded to the old paradigm when momentum is gathering for change. A person may find it physically impossible to see the world in any other way due to their long held beliefs, making the new paradigm incomprehensible to them... completely nonsensical.

In shifting paradigms, one goes from seeing the world in one way to the same world transforming before one's eyes... a total Gestalt shift... a complete transformation of perception. When gaping holes are personally exposed in a person's current paradigm, the tendency for their entire belief system to collapse upon itself is almost inescapable."

He looked down at the floor below him and spoke into his chest, his massive hand rubbing his furrowed brow.

"I guess it's also traumatic for those who find themselves adopting a new paradigm too early, as such early adopters are equally wedded to their new viewpoint. They couldn't go back even if they wanted to." He let out a short sigh and looked over at the kettle, its slow rumble gradually increasing in intensity.

"Are there any paradigm shifts that are commonly known?" Josh asked.

"Of course! These paradigm shifts, or revolutions, are evidenced throughout history, with a recently famous example being that of the shift from Newton's view of the world to that of Einstein's. Einstein's vision of the universe was revolutionary as it conflicted with fundamental axioms of the Newtonian Theory, giving us a completely different way of looking at the world.

We went from a world of absolute space and time, to one of relativity, with the main constant left being the speed of light. And the amazing thing about Einstein is that he did this all without physical experiments or empirical evidence. He relied totally on 'thought' experiments and his belief in the ultimate beauty and symmetry of his mathematical description of the universe. From these mental excursions he came up with the Special and General Theory of Relativity."

"No evidence? So what reasons did he give to support his new way of thinking?" Josh asked.

"Well, as I said, he argued for the inherent beauty of his Theory, holding a firm conviction that he saw the universe in the 'correct' light and that everyone else would catch up!"

"And they did obviously," Josh commented.

"Of course. However, at the time there was no experimental justification to switch paradigms. Indeed, the absolute success of Newtonian theory to accurately describe and predict phenomena on the earth really gave one no reason to ever shift away from it. However, its limitations were exposed when dealing with the very large and the very small. A famous experiment performed by Sir Arthur Eddington in 1919 during an eclipse proved the 'validity' of relativity over Newtonian physics once and for all. Einstein's Theory accurately predicted the relative position of a distant star and the amount our sun's gravity warped the light as it travelled to earth. Newtonian Theory did not."

The kettle was now ferociously boiling, awaiting collection. Will carefully filled the teapot with water and joined Josh at the table, pouring two cups. Josh took a small sip of his steaming brew.

"Newtonian physics is what I am sure I was taught in high school – rules like speed is equal to distance divided by time?" Josh said.

"Yes, of course you were." Will said. "The simplicity and ease of use of Newtonian Theory and its accuracy when dealing with macroscopic earth bound problems means that it is an invaluable instrumental theory, used and taught throughout the world, but it's not an accurate description of how the universe behaves as a whole."

"You mentioned the very large and..."

"...the very small, yes. Well, that was another matter entirely, even for Einstein. General relativity is superb for dealing with great distances over large time scales with its description of a curved, four dimensional space-time continuum. However, with the very small we have come to find that some very strange things happen that were not predicted by anyone, including Einstein. This is the world of Quantum Theory, the most paradoxical and most successful physical scientific theory to have ever existed."

"So Einstein was wrong about the atomic world?"

"Actually Einstein's paper on the photoelectric effect that he published in 1905 planted the seeds for what was to become known as Quantum Theory. He was one of its founders, and could have been one of its early pioneers had he been able to accept the strange atomic world that was gradually being uncovered."

"So this was another paradigm shift?"

"Exactly. Only this time, the shift was one from classical physics... generally held to include both Newtonian and Einsteinian Theories... to Quantum physics. Einstein, with one of the greatest minds to have ever existed, could not accept the findings from this bizarre emerging science and spent much of his latter days trying to disprove it!"

"That makes no sense to me. If he was one of its founders, he should have championed it!" Josh exclaimed.

"Josh, it's not that easy. The findings of Quantum theory are so logically unpalatable that no one would accept it if it wasn't experimentally proven time and time again. I suspect with the weight of experimental evidence now present to support Quantum theory, Einstein would have eventually come to accept it, as have all scientists. You know though, the funny thing is that if it wasn't for Einstein's vigorous opposition, Quantum Theory wouldn't have become established as quickly as it did!"

"What do you mean?" Josh asked.

"Einstein constantly challenged the early proponents of Quantum Theory with thought experiments he had produced, trying to prove some logical inconsistency. This forced those early adopters to rebut these challenges, further elucidating the overall theory and strengthening it from further attack."

"So why did Einstein have such a problem?" Josh asked.

"Well, I think for a couple of reasons. Firstly, from a question of beauty, Quantum physics is not a classically beautiful theorem mathematically – postulating multitudes of different particles within a highly complex, messy framework. The other objection that he had was a philosophical one, with Quantum Theory replacing the idea of cause and effect with one of probability – the origin of the Einstein quote 'God does not play dice'."

"But I thought that Einstein was the greatest scientist the world had ever seen? How could he disagree with the emerging scientific consensus, given the evidence being uncovered?"

"For two reasons. One, most of the experimental verification of Quantum Theory occurred after his death in 1955 as technology hadn't evolved sufficiently enough before then. But, the second reason is exactly what I was talking about before, people become overly committed to their paradigm and have great difficulties letting go, due to reasons beyond cold rationality. His whole professional life was built on his ground-breaking discoveries, especially that of General Relativity. Imagine how hard it would be to let go of a paradigm you devised, that revolutionized the world and cemented your place in history as one of the greatest scientific thinkers of all time?"

The sun had finally set beneath the horizon, with its residual glow now also fading for another day. Steam continued to rise from their teacups, as the crisp evening air gradually decreased in temperature.

"So why is Quantum Theory so strange?" Josh asked, warming his hands around his cup as he swallowed another mouthful of tea.

"Well, for starters, when looking at an atom, we previously thought they were made up of protons and neutrons that resided in the nucleus. Electrons then circle the nucleus, in various numbers and various layers, or 'shells'. The amount of protons, neutrons, electrons and then consequently electron shells, could be illustrated by an element's number and position on the periodic table. These particles were all said to be fundamental, the building blocks of all matter. With the discovery of Quantum Theory we realized we were wrong in a couple of different ways."

"How?" Josh asked.

"We still think that electrons are fundamental particles, but protons and neutrons are made up of much smaller particles, called quarks. There are six types of quarks, known as flavors, which all have electric and color charge, spin and mass."

"What are you talking about? Flavors and colors?"

"Yeah I know, interesting names, yes? I think they tend to confuse matters for the layman but that is what we are stuck with!" he said with a chuckle.

"However where we really had no idea was how events in the atomic world are just plain *strange*. They defy all logic that we have learned through observation in our lives and, frankly, would never have been believed if we hadn't validated their existence over and over again. A beginning to this weirdness is seen in the Heisenberg Uncertainty Principle."

Will took a long sip of his tea.

"Now as I said before, we believed that electrons orbited the nucleus of an atom in shells, but we visualized this orbit in much the same way as we perceive the orbits of the planets in our solar system. All planets orbit around our star, the Sun, at fixed distances and at fixed speeds. Thus, one can make accurate predictions about the distance and speed at any one time. We found that this assumption about the atomic world was fundamentally wrong. Whenever we tried to accurately determine the speed of an electron, we could do so. But if we tried to simultaneously determine its location, we were unable to!

Conversely, if we wanted to determine the location of an electron, we could do so to a high degree of accuracy, but found we could not know the speed at the same time!"

"But how can that be possible? If you can locate an object at all, you can obviously work out how fast it is going as you are watching it. You just time how long it takes the object to travel across a known distance."

"Very true, in the macroscopic world. But not quite the same in the quantum world. When you measure the position of an atom, the act of measuring alters the atom's momentum, affecting any accurate determination of speed. Conversely, when you measure its speed, the act of measurement affects its position."

Josh sat silently trying to bend his mind around Will's words as he continued.

"In addition to this, there are all kinds of strange phenomena. Particles disappearing and reappearing at random, often in different places."

"You mean like teleportation?"

"Exactly. Two single particles can also exist in two locations at the same time!"

"What! How can this be possible?"

"This is illustrated in the thought experiment of the paradox of Schrödinger's cat: Imagine a cat trapped in a box. The box is sealed with no possibility of observing the cat from the outside. Now imagine that in the box there is a vial of toxic gas, with the opening of the vial controlled by a switch. This switch is set by the monitoring of a radio isotope that has a fifty percent probability of decay over a certain period of time. If the decay is registered, the vial is opened and the cat dies. If it isn't, the vial remains closed and the cat lives. Now my question for you, is the cat alive or dead?"

"I have no idea. I would have to look in the box!"

"Ha!" Will exclaimed, slapping the table. "Well you're actually partly right."

"Partly?" Josh asked.

"If the box has remained sealed, and no information about the cat being alive or dead has escaped the box, *the cat is both alive and dead at the same time.*"

"What!?" Josh exclaimed. "How can that be possible? Just because it isn't known by someone doesn't make it any less true that the cat either died or lived."

"Actually, in the quantum world, it does. The cat is in a state of *quantum superposition*. As there is a fifty per cent chance of it being alive and being dead, there are two equally likely possibilities for the future of the cat that are both equally real until someone observes the result. It is the act of observation that causes the superposition state to break down and one of the probabilistic paths to become 'real'."

"So without the act of observation, all possibilities exist of an event happening?"

"Yes." Will hesitated. "Well, kind of. That is what is required under the Copenhagen interpretation of the implications of Quantum mechanics, also known as the Standard Model. It is the most commonly held view in the world but it is not the only way to look at the world. And to be honest, none of the interpretations have any hard evidence to be accepted as fact over each other. All the different interpretations have their adherents in the scientific community, all adequately explain the philosophical consequences of what we know but each entail their own bizarre consequences. Take for example the many worlds explanation.

In the case of Schrodinger's cat there is no superposition, as both possibilities are actually realized in two different universes! Every time the universe is faced with a choice between multiple events, the universe multiplies to realize each event in question. So literally every second, countless universes are being created fulfilling the myriad of possibilities presented with each moment."

"That seems unbelievable."

"Yes, quite. That interpretation violates one of the most sacred assumptions of modern science, Ockham's Razor. This states that when postulating a scientific theory, one must not postulate entities unnecessarily."

"The simplest explanation tends to be the right one?"

"A rough paraphrasing of the principle, yes." Will replied.

"So you can see that the many worlds model does seem to violate this, postulating an infinite number of universes to explain reality.

The funny thing is, Quantum Theory itself would fail this test spectacularly if it wasn't for its experimental support. It is one of the most convoluted in science, with the many multitudes of 'fundamental' particles discovered through work with particle accelerators around the globe and all the metaphysical baggage one must take on when considering the actual, real world implications of the Theory."

Josh frowned as a worrying thought filled his mind.

"Hang on a minute. With the standard interpretation of the theory being reliant on observation, how can science ever be objective? Aren't you part of the experiment when you're observing it?" Josh asked.

Will nodded approvingly.

"Quite the quandary for scientists I can assure you. Modern science has in part been a project designed to remove the belief in the central importance of man in the universe, and it seems that its most successful theory has placed man squarely back in the center again!"

Darkness now firmly surrounding them, Josh and Will were barely visible to each other across the table. In the absence of the moon and any significant light pollution, a magnificent view of the surrounding universe was on full display above them.

"Hang on a second, let me get us some light..."

Will stood up and slowly made his way back to his outdoor kitchen, producing two large candles. Lighting them both and placing them in the center of the table, their conversation was now illuminated by warm candlelight, dancing slowly in the surrounding breeze.

"So how is this paradox dealt with by scientists?" Josh asked.

"One word. Denial! In general, the scientific community prefers not to consider most of the philosophical implications of its theories nowadays. Once upon a time that was the purpose of science, to better understand our universe and the meaning of our place in it. But somewhere along the way we became lost and caught up with all the neat ways we could manipulate the physical world to fill up our lives."

"So, you are saying that science doesn't care about the why anymore, because it gave us technology?"

"No. I'm saying that no one seems to care anymore about the why, because we are all so distracted, in part, by our modern technological trinkets. Why care about what Quantum theory really means when its application enables flat screen TV's, microwaves and computers all to be possible."

"So why do you care?"

"Who says I do!" Will shouted back.

"So why do you live out here by yourself then?" Josh asked, "And why did Zach come out here to see you then, for a lesson on the history of science?"

"I suspect that Lloyd sent Zach out here to talk to me as I had had a profound paradigm shift in my life and experienced great loss. Maybe he thought I could relate to Zach in some way."

"Who died?" Josh asked.

"Well, nobody died, other than the person that was previously me. Not something that I would have chosen to happen and I can't even say if I had the choice again, knowing what I know now, if I would do the same."

After pouring the remaining contents of the teapot into their cups, Will stood up again and walked over to the stove, turning the dial to reheat the water in the kettle.

"The saying 'ignorance is bliss' is not without merit, especially when the veil of ignorance is lifted only to reveal an infinite amount of new questions..." Will said.

"So, what happened to you?" Josh asked.

Will leaned on the kitchen bench and tilted his head towards the stars. Grasping the wooden edge with his hands, he steadied himself for the verbal journey he was about to begin. He returned eye contact with Josh, inhaled deeply and started to speak.

"Once upon a time, I was a normal scientist.

I was successful in my field of particle physics and well respected by my friends and colleagues. I really loved my career and would say that I was a happy person. I had a wife, a fellow scientist that I loved and was planning to start a family with. My research focus at the time was in Quantum chromodynamics, looking at the interactions between quarks and gluons."

"Huh?" Josh exclaimed.

"A fascinating area but not important for my story. Like most physicists, I was content to solve the mathematical problems presented to me, not at all focused on the greater philosophical implications of my research or my field.

Anyway, one day I was attending a function at a colleague's home, and I happened to engage in a discussion with this 10 year old boy, Steven. I was asking him about his school and he replied by asking me about my work.

"Why are you a scientist?" Steven asked. I knelt down in front of him so I could speak to Steven face to face.

"Well, I guess because I was always good at math and enjoyed solving problems," I answered.

"What kind of problems do you solve?" he asked.

"I study things that are very very small. The tiny building blocks that make up everything... you, me, our planet, the entire universe!"

Steven sat there in pensive silence for a moment, his lower lip protruding as creases formed on his small forehead.

"Why is there something and not nothing?" asked Steven.

I grinned at his question, thinking of the innate curiosity that children are blessed with. As I began to try and formulate a satisfactory answer, my mind was awash with equations, all describing some part of the known universe but all equally unsatisfactory for the question at hand. At that moment a small girl ran up to Steven, giggling and whispering something in his ear. He laughed too, both running off hand in hand. He turned as he was leaving and waved goodbye. I slowly stood up and waved back.

With no answer immediately apparent at the time, I brushed aside his enquiry as that of a naive child.

I could not imagine that such an innocent question could plant the seed of my paradigm shift."

Will's eyes closed as he revisited that moment in time, slowly shaking his head in disbelief as he considered the seemingly inconsequential question responsible for the last 15 years of his life.

"Try as I might, I could not get Steven's question out of my mind. After that day, I began to ask questions of my discipline that I had never thought to ask and was increasingly unsatisfied with the answers. Greater metaphysical questions of existence, purpose and meaning arose in me. I figured that being a physicist, studying the essence of matter as we knew it, I would be equipped to deal with such enquiries. But time and time again, I found any excursion to my toolbox of mathematical formulae that had served me so well as woefully inadequate. My wife and colleagues were all convinced that I was overworked and needed a break, or I wouldn't be asking such ridiculous questions that I could never find answers to. I was also surprised when one of my fellow professors pulled me aside one day to tell me that I needed religion! He explained that he had effectively compartmentalized his belief systems, one for physics and modern science and one for the foundational questions of life, all conveniently answered by his ancient scripture."

The boiling kettle again reached its crescendo, spewing forth its torrent of steam. Will returned to the table and refilled the teapot, continuing his story as he went.

"I could appreciate his need for this belief, but I found the whole system less convincing than anything I had found in science, replacing the questions that I had with a blind belief in some ancient dogma.

Physics with all the promise of the 'Grand Unified Theory' to finally unlock the keys to everything seemed as distant as ever. Possibilities such as String Theory, once a great hope, now seemed more like a mere mathematical curiosity, failing one of science's most basic criteria, testability. More worrying still, I had come to realize that even if the GUT was discovered, answers to these questions of existence and our purpose within it would still remain elusive. All these realizations left me feeling unsatisfied with my life. Problems that once would have left me intellectually curious for months now seemed like trivialities, as did conversations with my colleagues. This soon also became the case with my wife, with us drifting further and further apart."

Will leant across the table and poured Josh, and then himself, a fresh cup of tea.

"Why didn't you do anything to stop it?" Josh interjected.

"Ah, you act like I had a choice in all this. One doesn't usually set out to change one's worldview. A paradigm can become dislodged easily if the right external influence is applied, just like the strongest structure can be toppled if the right leverage is applied against a critical point. This is especially so if it is weak at its foundations already."

"How can you say that modern science is weak?"

"Because it ignores one basic fact about humanity: man's inherent spiritual essence. I had been on a quest to answer the questions that life presented to me since I was a child and when the most fundamental of those questions was raised, I found that my life long career in physics did not have any real answers for me."

"Wow," Josh said. "So what did you do next?"

"One day I was walking across campus, particularly down about everything that was happening to me. Feeling isolated and alone, I noticed a sign for a meditation class being held that evening. I have no idea what sparked my curiosity, if it was its bright orange color that caught my eye or the photograph of a pink lotus flower that was featured in its center. Whatever it was, I made the decision on the spot to attend. So that evening I found myself participating in a guided meditation with a group of students. After that... everything changed."

"Just by meditating? How?" Josh asked.

"It was like a veil was lifted from my eyes and myself, my real inner self, finally felt some peace for the first time since all this had occurred.

I walked home with a beaming smile. Cooked a large delicious meal and made love to my wife. She couldn't understand what had come over me but she was overjoyed, thinking that she had her old husband back. Unfortunately for us, that was not the case, but I will never forget that night.

I continued to go to the meditation class and felt more and more at peace with myself.

However, I was less and less interested in work and it became increasingly difficult even to feign interest.

I became a voracious reader of all things concerned with meditation, exploring the Transcendental Meditation Movement, Zen Buddhism and even some forms of esoteric Christianity and the mystical form of Islam, Sufism. I knew that this was the path that my life now had to take, so I quit my job. I was already so far behind in my work and ostracized from my fellow professors that I think they all were thankful when I finally left voluntarily. However, me leaving work was the final straw for my wife. My things were packed up neatly beside the front door with a note asking me to leave when I returned home one evening."

"That's unacceptable" Josh said, his voice raised slightly betraying his own recently scorched feelings. "How could she not support you?"

"It wasn't her fault but at the time I thought much the same thing. I felt she was *obligated* to support me through my life change. But she didn't have the conceptual faculties available to get her head around my new belief system and why I was doing what I was doing. If the roles were reversed, I have no doubt I would have done the same thing. My behavior was incommensurable to her. I was no longer the man she fell in love with. As she had not changed concurrently with me, it was only natural that it was our time to part. Divorce is often seen as a great evil by many people. However, in many cases, a greater harm would be to stay together when two people have grown apart so much that their differences are irreconcilable. One can choose to live an unhappy life together, as that is what 'society' or 'church' may deem appropriate, or, one can make an attempt at a happy life apart. The psychic damage one can inflict on children by remaining in the same house while constantly fighting, verbally or physically, is usually far greater than any harm caused by living apart."

"So you have no regrets then?" Josh asked.

"Regrets? Do I regret making the choices that I did? No, insofar as when I actually made my own choices. But do I wish that my belief system was not so fundamentally altered? Sometimes..."

"How can you say that? Don't you believe that you are closer to your 'truth'?"

"Yes. But what is 'truth' anyway, and what is the purpose of life? I have had many significant insights since that time and I generally enjoy my life out here living with nature, but would I have been happier if all this hadn't occurred? If

I had remained happy with my world view and thus happy in my career and marriage? Sometimes, I suspect, yes..."

They both sat back in their chairs, pondering the implications of what Will had just said. Questions of purpose and happiness in our short lives are seldom answered for many. Even if *some* answers are found, one may be disappointed that a purposeful, happy life remains elusive. Despite these difficult questions, both Josh and Will were sharing a simple pleasure, sitting in the cool night air, their hot beverages stoked a satisfying inner furnace. Will leaned towards Josh in his chair.

"I tell all this to you as I see you on the precipice of where I once was. And once you travel too far there is no turning back even if you choose to. Your old life will forever be lost to you. Zach's old life was lost with the death of his sister, so there was already no turning back for him."

"My old life evaporated on that plane," Josh confessed. "I would love to go back to 'normal' and pick up where I left off. But I've already tried to and there's nothing left for me there. Finding Zach is the only thing that feels right to me now. All I hope is that he can help me when I do. I can't live like this." Josh said, a hint of desperation coloring his voice.

"Okay then. It seems that you have been forced onto your path as much as Zach was. I hope that I can give you some help in finding him, but I must warn you, I haven't spoken to him since he left here."

"Whatever you could tell me would be appreciated."

"After he left me he travelled to a spiritual retreat center near Sedona in the Arizona desert. A place I lived for a while after my divorce. They helped me greatly. I hope they do the same for you."

Will produced a pen and some paper from his pocket and wrote down the details of the retreat center, handing them to Josh.

"Thank you Will. Being able to put a name and a concept to my 'paradigm shift' makes me feel like I did the right thing coming to see you."

"You're welcome. Try to view what's happened thus far as a good thing, Josh. What has happened has happened, and cannot be undone. Your journey will be much easier to manage if you can truly accept your past and shift your focus positively.

Easier said than done, I know, but do your best. It will be more than worth it."

They both stood as Josh prepared to leave. Exchanging their final farewells, Josh turned to head toward his car.

Will called out to him.

"Just remember Josh, how can we *really* know anything other than our own mind?"

chapter 5

After the 15 hour flight from Melbourne to Los Angeles, Josh picked up the Mercedes Benz rental car that was to take him to the Enso retreat center in Arizona. Typing the address details into the navigation system, a German accented female proceeded to tell him to turn right in three hundred feet, the first of many words he would hear from his only travel companion on the long drive. Josh began with great anticipation on his journey. Although his efforts to find Zach had not yielded any definitive results, the many insights he had gained into his own personal journey had proven to be invaluable. A return to his previous existence still seemed untenable, but he was sufficiently distracted by the task at hand to prevent lingering thoughts of the remainder of his life. In addition, he had not had an official 'holiday' for over five years so his body was beginning to relax and enjoy his sudden well earned respite.

After ten hours behind the wheel, Josh drew closer to his destination as he traversed the great rugged expanse that is Arizona. The rock formations he was encountering seem to be carved by giants, the red sandstone mountains framing panoramic views everywhere he looked. As the sun tracked its familiar path, the desert colors morphed continuously, ensuring the view never remained the same. The magical sense of presence he felt driving through the desolate rocky countryside made the time spent driving effortless. Indeed, after his 'driving meditation', he felt relaxed and revived upon his arrival in Sedona.

Since the 'harmonic convergence' of 1987, Sedona was home to a plethora of New Age merchants, tourists and seekers of all kinds. They had all come to gain energy and insight from the 'spiritual vortices' that were present there surrounding the township. Seeing the commerce generated from these beliefs as he drove through the town, he was skeptical that this was all nothing more than a money driven exercise, efficiently fuelling the financial coffers of the town. Despite these misgivings he could feel an ineffable presence in the surrounding area, although he didn't have the vocabulary to describe these feelings.

Nevertheless, there was no debating the views. Nestled in the lower end of Oak Creek Canyon, the spectacular natural rock formations he had been observing during his drive appeared to concentrate around this unique little town. Like so many words in our verbose world, 'spectacular' had lost some meaning through overuse but couldn't be more apt in describing Josh's view at that moment.

He stopped at the local visitors' guide center, asked for directions to the Enso retreat and continued on his journey. The retreat was located two miles west of Sedona on an expansive piece of land.

Turning left into the clearly marked drive, Josh was immediately greeted by two massive totem poles standing either side of the entry road. Slowing down for a closer inspection, he noticed their intricate detail was clearly not a depiction of Native American craftsmanship. Religious iconography from all the lands of the earth sat together in a harmonious montage. Jesus supporting Mohammad, the Buddha dining with Moses, cultures and traditions intertwined around the cylindrical columns. As the beautiful structures faded into the distance behind him, he was to soon see more thoughtful depictions of unity throughout the retreat.

Josh travelled down the gently winding drive, climbing a final rise to reveal the center's main grounds. He was surprised by what he saw. The road formed a large circle in front of the main building, surrounding a lush flowerbed of deep purple and brilliant white flowers. The flower arrangement formed a large Yin/Yang symbol, planted on a slight incline to welcome new retreat dwellers as they arrived. The main building was a Victorian style gothic mansion. Made of large red sandstone blocks over a century ago by a wealthy local family, it stood in stark contrast to the buildings adjacent to it. To the left was a large smooth pyramid, standing at over 40 feet high, with a massive dome structure standing to the right. All were made from the same red sandstone. He could see in the distance other unusual geometric forms, all in contradiction, but all settled in harmony, all carved from the same rock.

He traversed the circular road and pulled up at the entrance, with a valet entirely clothed in white taking his keys and driving his car away for storage.

Josh slung his backpack over his shoulder and walked through the large wooden entrance, proceeding to the check-in area. He soon noticed that the white uniform of the valet was worn by everyone he saw. Josh didn't dwell on the strange attire but instead surrendered to the serene atmosphere. Light instrumental music played through hidden speakers, with fragrant incense flavoring the air.

Everything seemed completely removed from the modern world outside. Josh felt like he had just stepped through a vortex into a tranquil alternate reality.

Standing at the check-in counter he was greeted by a short, middle-aged woman with a beaming smile. Josh introduced himself.

"So Josh, is this your first time staying with us?" she asked.

"Yes, it is." he answered.

"Lovely. Well allow me to explain the rules that govern the retreat. Now you must agree to abide by these if you want to be a part of our community. Some may seem strange, but allow me to explain..."

"Uhhh, okay," Josh replied nervously.

"Firstly, I have to ask you to check in all of your possessions."

"What!" he cried.

"Don't worry, they'll be kept safe for you until you leave. Everything you will need on your stay will be provided for you."

"What for? What kind of place is this?"

"Some of our guests do find this initially difficult. Our egos are so bound up in our possessions and the garments that we drape over ourselves. Thus, it is natural for the mind to rise up in anger at the thought of sacrificing this part of our identity for a time."

She pointed over at a carved wooden door behind him.

"A change room is over there. Here's a bag to put your things in and here are your robes. Let me know if they don't fit properly."

She handed him the bag and his new attire. Josh took them both without further protest, despite a lingering unease with the situation he had found himself in.

"What size shoe are you?" she asked.

"Size 12," Josh replied.

She handed him a pair of white slippers. His hands now full, he walked over into the change room and shut the door behind him.

"What kind of bizarre cult have I just walked into?" he thought to himself as he removed his clothes and donned the white robes.

He stood before the full length mirror in the change room, draped in white. He still felt very strange, like he was doing something very wrong by abandoning his clothes. Paradoxically, he also felt a sensation of calm while gazing upon his image. He placed his old clothes in the provided bag, slipped on his new shoes and walked back to the reception desk.

"Here you go," he said, handing over the last evidence of his life outside the retreat. "So you didn't explain to me why?"

She smiled back at him with kind eyes.

"Here at the Enso center we have created a sanctuary from the company brands and logos that permeate our everyday existence. Not a single brand or logo is on display, except for an occasional reference to the retreat itself. We have done this in an effort to aid the calming of the mind by removing one of the main distractions of the modern world – the ever present talons of the marketing industry. We are trying to help 'turn off' the consumer part of ourselves that has been fed and nourished throughout our lives, so we can concentrate on more important matters."

"Hang on!" he objected. "Without us all as consumers, we wouldn't live in the world that we know today."

"Very true," she agreed, "but one could argue both positively and negatively for the statement you just made."

"What are you talking about? We all know the world has problems, it always has. But we enjoy a much better life now because of consumerism."

"I do agree that there's no doubt that improvements in the quality of life have been dramatic for sections of the planet over the past century or so. But the mindless consumerism that goes on in most of our lives on a daily basis does not seem to be contributing individually in any meaningful way. At best, it is only able to provide fleeting moments of happiness that are soon replaced by an inner emptiness. Time and again we are driven to temporarily fill this void by the purchase of some new product, and around and around we go..." she said, holding her index finger in the air and spinning it round like a top.

He knew he had been guilty of this. "But what is really wrong with comfort shopping? I know it can bring me out of a bad mood."

"The main problem is that it doesn't address the underlying spiritual malaise that many of us feel, only providing a temporary Band-Aid. At our retreat we are attempting to free up some space in our cluttered minds to find some real peace, to restore some balance. Removing the constant salesman that pitches to us consciously or unconsciously throughout our day can help us gain some freedom over our habitual thoughts. It is something that we hope you can take back into your world, to help you to function better and be less influenced by marketing when back in your normal life."

This discussion was increasingly dipping into 'new age' babble to Josh, with words like 'peace' and 'balance' tossed around causing him to mentally retreat, with fortifying walls going up in his head.

Sensing this, she smiled again and said, "These things usually become clearer after you have stayed with us for a while. I hope you enjoy your time here with us."

She leant over and gave Josh a hug. He would usually find affection from a complete stranger socially awkward, but he felt such a warmth from her embrace that he didn't want to let go. As he was leaving he asked her if she knew Zach, but as she has only been working at the center for five years, she did not.

After leaving the reception area and finding his room, he was to be treated with a massage to begin his stay. When he arrived at his massage room he was informed that the practitioner had gone over time with their current client and was asked if he would mind waiting in the adjoining courtyard.

The courtyard was framed by red sandstone walls, all encrusted with vines and moss. Life was abundant, bursting forth from every possible opening. He walked along a paved section towards a tall fountain. The fountain was made of black tile fashioned in the shape of a pagoda, with water cascading down through the multi leveled structure. The fountain was encircled by a stone seating area where his eye was instinctively drawn to the beautiful Sophia.

She was consumed by a book and didn't notice Josh's approach, her straight black hair hanging down to partially mask her face. Her white robes took on an angelic quality as they performed their task of covering her delicate frame. Josh was entranced and proceeded to interrupt her study.

"Excuse me, would you mind if I sat down?" he asked.

She raised her blue eyes from her text, parting her hair and running it behind her ears to reveal her perfectly proportioned face, rose tinted cheeks and full lips.

She thought about the question momentarily, allowing the corners of her mouth to convey a smile and responded. "Sure. But I'm afraid I won't be much company. I want to get through this chapter before my afternoon class with Roger."

Josh nodded and sat down. "No problem. Pretend I'm not even here."

He crossed his legs and began to feign interest in his surroundings, while plotting what to say next. His previous years of experience in manipulating beautiful women to satisfy his own sexual urges had again possessed his thoughts, now switching over to run purely on instinct. The biological urge to spread his seed, having been fed so well for many years, took central command of his faculties.

He decided that as always the key to slaying a beautiful woman was confidence and the front that you don't need her, so he started with a subtle 'neg'.

"I'm sorry to interrupt you again but I'm compelled to ask. You've got such a beautiful face. Why do you choose to hide it with all that hair? You'd look really stunning with a shorter style…"

Sophie reached down next to her, picked up her bookmark and marked her page.

"I'm sorry, what was your name?"

"I'm Josh, and you are?"

"I'm Sophie."

Josh put out his hand which she firmly grasped, both still keeping eye contact.

"A pleasure to meet you." Josh said.

"So Josh, do you ever give any real thought to how your words impact on those around you?"

He was taken aback by the question. There was no anger displayed in her face but the direct nature of her enquiry had taken him by surprise.

Lost for words, he could only manage an indignant, "Uhhh..."

Sophie continued, "For example, imagine a situation where a guy noticed a girl he was attracted to, so he went up and approached her.

Now in order to disarm her, he said hello, and then proceeded to launch a veiled insult at her..."

"But I didn't mean..." Josh began.

She cut him off, "Yes you did. But please let me finish."

"Now such an insult could be taken by the girl in a number of ways. Of course, the boy hasn't considered these possibilities, as he is focused on trying to cultivate an attraction with the girl. But those poorly chosen words have got the capacity to extend into the future and contribute towards ruining her day, week, or even month or year."

Josh drew breath, preparing to rebut her statement but Sophie raised her hand to silence him.

"Now the boy, after talking to her some more, may lose interest..."

"Now that's doubtful." Josh interjected.

"...and leave after a few minutes. But the girl, due to past issues still resonating strongly with her, may replay the ill-chosen words, magnifying their power, reinforcing her limiting beliefs."

"Hang on," Josh became defensive. "Surely people have responsibility for their own thoughts and beliefs. 'The girl' had the choice to ignore the comments and not let them affect her."

"I agree. We all do have responsibility for our thoughts and actions. But that does not mean in this instance that she had any real choice about how she acted. Unless one has cultivated presence in their lives, one is fated to react to events, effectively unable to choose how to act."

She paused a moment to consider her words.

"I understand someone who is obviously as poorly educated as yourself may not understand this," she stated.

Josh felt pangs of physical pain in his body with blood rushing to his face. His mind quickly stirred into action with a vitriolic roar. "How dare you! I can assure you I'm better educated than you and all the people in this hippy commune!"

Sophie's eyes smiled and she gently reached over and held Josh's hand.

"As I said, before one has cultivated presence, you will find that one often doesn't have any real choice in how they think, speak or act."

Josh was instantly disarmed with the touch of her hand and the compassion in her voice.

"Josh Black, we're ready for you now," sounded a voice from the treatment area.

"It was lovely to meet you Josh," Sophie said, "I hope you find what you need during your stay here."

With that, Sophie reopened her book and was again quickly immersed in its contents.

"Nice to meet you too," Josh said as he stood, somewhat bewildered from the unusual interaction he just experienced.

After the massage and a short nap, Josh arrived at his next appointment. He was scheduled to see his retreat mentor. They were tasked to take care of Josh during his stay and to ensure he received maximum benefit from his time away from the world outside. He arrived at Stephanie's office early and sat waiting at her door on an old wooden chair, its cushion covered in faded brown cotton. He was already feeling quite relaxed and rejuvenated after his massage and sleep, better than he had felt in some time. Thoughts of Zach and his personal crisis were temporarily absent as he waited and enjoyed just sitting for a brief, fleeting period.

The approach of Stephanie brought him back to the immediate world.

"Well, it looks like you're already making some progress. Great!" said Stephanie as she put out her hand to shake Josh's. Not sure of what she meant but still in the residual glow of his mini meditation, he responded with an enthusiastic, "Thanks!" He immediately chastised himself for such over enthusiasm and was quickly returned to his normal state of being.

She gave him a kind smile with a flicker of recognition of the change in his inner state. "Please come in and take a seat."

Stephanie's office was a small, uncluttered space, with redwood furniture. Her desk had a slim line black computer screen with a mouse and keyboard below and no cords present. There was a photo of a giant Buddha statue on the wall and a large bookcase neatly filled with books.

One corner contained a shrine with various offerings and statues including a large Buddha seated at its center. There was an assortment of candles scattered throughout, which she started to light after entering the room.

"Now Josh, why don't you tell me what brings you to us?" she said as she finished lighting the last candle, sitting down in her oversized reclining chair.

Josh proceeded to tell the story of his near-death experience, ensuing personal crisis, and his quest to find his old friend, recounting the main events of the past month leading up to that point. She listened intently during his retelling, absorbing his tale with all her being. After he finished, Josh let out a large sigh, again sinking into feelings of despair and hopelessness after the detailed recollection of his current predicament.

"Wow," Stephanie replied, "that's great! Do you feel lucky?"

"What! Are you serious? Lucky would be the last thing I'm feeling," Josh answered.

"Really? Well then, luck is all a matter of perspective now, isn't it?"

Josh began to feel familiar waves of anger and frustration come over him. Blood rapidly flowed to his face, his breathing, perspiration and heart rate all began to increase upon the perceived attack.

"What the hell would you know?" he said as his voice became louder. "My life is in ruins! So to answer your question, NO, I have no idea what I am doing here!"

Stephanie sat calmly and waited for him to finish. "People wait their entire lives to have an experience such as yours, Josh. They attend retreats like ours, meditate every day, and they may never be blessed with what has been given to you."

Josh sat in a pained silence, glaring back at her.

"Were you happy before your plane crash?" she asked.

"Of course! I had many people that admired and respected me, countless women that wanted to be with me and a job that most people would kill for. Basically, I had everything anyone could ever want. So of course I was happy!"

Stephanie leaned forward in her chair, "If you can only reply by listing things you had or that other people desired from you, I think you may have forgotten what happiness is."

"What would you know? I have no idea what you're talking about?" Josh replied, becoming increasingly defensive.

"What I am talking about is that the trauma you have been through has helped loosen the mask that you have held up to the world for your entire adult life. The reason why you can't go back to 'normal' is that you have seen beyond the artifice that is the vacuous existence of materialism and the constant gratification of your ego. Once you have seen, you cannot un-see. You need to accept the change that has occurred and move forward to find meaning in your life again."

Josh looked on incredulously, "Accept the change? Ha! Easier said than done! What do you think I'm doing here!"

Stephanie continued, "Any significant change in one's life will bring about sensations of being uncomfortable, especially in the period of transition. This is a necessary part of venturing out into the unknown and forging a new path. But the one thing that will exacerbate any ill feelings is resistance to that change. You didn't consciously bring about this new state of being, however, I believe unconsciously you have been living out of alignment with your true self for some time, with your spirit crying out for such a transformation, for such an opportunity..."

"So you are saying I brought this on myself? I brought a plane crash on myself!" Josh asked with disbelief.

"No. I am saying that your authentic self took advantage of the circumstances that were presented to it. You didn't have to react the way you did to your accident. But you did react this way, so now it's time to face your new reality and work with it."

"The only thing that has made me come anywhere near acceptance of all this is the thought of finding Zach," Josh said.

"This is understandable. You are reaching back to a time in your life where it was normal to be living in alignment with your inner principles. Trying to reach out to someone who inspired and motivated you do to this makes perfect sense.

However, I do caution you in putting all your hopes for salvation in finding your friend. We can all assist each other in our individual life journey, but ultimately each of us must seek our own truth."

Josh moved nervously in his seat, unsettled by her statement. He quickly changed the topic, "So what are you going to do to help me in my 'life journey'?"

Stephanie smiled, "We are going to start with the basics and move on from there."

"The basics being..."

"Your body. The path to greater self-awareness all starts with a greater awareness of your body. What it needs, how it feels..."

"But I always thought that spiritual traditions sought to remove emphasis on the body, concentrating on the mind or spirit?"

"Yes, some do. But I'm sorry to say they do so to their detriment. It is a fundamental fact of the reality we inhabit that the body and mind share an intimate bond. Thus, positive changes in the mind can help effect positive change in the body, and vice versa. As the all too common 'monkey mind' is notoriously difficult to control, it is only logical to begin with an easier starting point - positive change within the body. These changes will help bring about a calmer mind that is then more receptive to higher spiritual training."

"You mean like exercise?"

"Kind of. Of course fitness is good, but the obsession with western fitness goals can bring about overexertion and harm to your body and mind. I was thinking about something more basic: your diet and digestive system. The first thing we will do is detoxify your body."

"Yeah, I've done one of them on the advice of a girl I used to see. I ate fruit and vegetables for a week while taking some vitamin supplements. I must admit I felt pretty good after it."

"I see. Well, this one is a little more intense," Stephanie began, "We are going to gradually decrease your intake of food, until you are on a juice fast for five days. You will be taking herbal supplements throughout this period that will help brush your intestinal tract clean, dislodging toxic debris from its walls."

"A juice fast?" Josh exclaimed. "You mean, only juice for five days?"

"And herbs. The herbal concoction you'll be taking will help you feel full. For example, you'll be taking Psyllium husk. It's an extremely fibrous material that absorbs fluid which will expand in your stomach, taking away any hunger pains."

"I appreciate you using the word 'pain', because that's what it sounds like..."

"You'll be fine and, believe me, you'll thank us after it."

With the sequence of surreal conversations he had had since his arrival, a brief juice diet did not seem all that strange anymore so he accepted the program with no further protest.

"Okay then, what's next?"

"Good," she replied, impressed with his sudden agreement, "During your detox phase, you'll also be receiving daily colonic irrigations."

"What! You are NOT putting anything up there!" Josh stated quickly, any brief acceptance quickly evaporating. He sat squirming in his chair, an exaggerated mental picture he held causing him to grimace.

"Fasting I can accept, but not that!"

"Josh, do you have any idea what you are carrying around in there with you? Take a look at this..."

Stephanie opened a desk drawer and removed a cream file folder. She proceeded to remove a large color photo and passed it to Josh.

"Oh my God! What is that?" Josh exclaimed. The photo was of a long brown-green substance that had the shape of an intestinal tract, with indents from folded rugae clearly pronounced along its slimy gelatinous surface. It was clearly solid as it was held up by a stick over an open toilet bowl.

"Are they someone's intestines?" Josh asked, passing the photo back away from view.

"No, Josh, that is what came out of me, after my third colonic, during the herbal fast you are about to undertake. It is called mucoid plaque which is basically built up toxic residue from all the junk I had consumed throughout my life."

"That's disgusting. And so you think that I have something similar in me?"

"Everyone that's come through our program has had some nasty substances released during this phase."

Josh's mind's eye made its way into his abdomen, visualizing similar material lining his digestive tube. Josh's perspective understandably shifted, "Well I don't care what you have to do, just get that out of me!"

Stephanie smiled, "That's the usual reaction after people are made aware of what they're carrying around inside them. Good."

She slid the photo back into the folder and replaced it in her desk.

"After you finish that stage, you'll be on a strict diet of organic fruit, vegetables and whole grains, most of which are grown right here on the retreat."

"Well, after the colonic, I don't see how that'll be a problem. What else will I be doing during all this?" he asked.

"During the detox phase, you'll have a daily deep tissue full body massage. This will work to reinforce the detox process, helping to move toxins from their places of storage ready for expulsion."

"Now that sounds more appealing!" Josh exclaimed.

"You will usually walk away from your massages feeling great, but a word of warning: the massages themselves can be quite painful at times, even emotional. Over the years our bodies become blocked and contorted due to the stresses and strains of our lives. Experiences of emotional trauma that we never really dealt with properly can become suppressed and locked deep within our bodies. Your prescribed diet, colonics and massages work synergistically to help unlock these repressed emotions, making space for them to arise, be felt and dissipate."

"But that makes no sense," Josh protested. "All one's emotions are experienced by the brain, the seat of our consciousness, as are all our memories. And I don't have any pent up trauma needing to be released, I was never abused as a child..."

"Emotional trauma does not need to be that extreme to be suppressed and held by the body. I would say from my brief time with you, someone that has lived out of alignment with their purpose for so many years would have been repressing emotional conflict on a daily basis. This all needs to be dealt with and released so you can move on effectively. This process has already started with you due to your recent trauma, hence the overwhelming nature of the emotions that have been bubbling up to the surface of your consciousness.

Every pang of guilt, sadness, anger, and grief you have brushed aside and not fully experienced is within you, weighing you down subconsciously like an anchor. Your previous response to this was to feed your ego with a sense of wealth or power. This only brought relief as the inflated ego could again mask these feelings, but they still remained intact, waiting in a growing line to be experienced."

"I still don't understand how massages are going to help with this. If one did indeed have such pent up emotions, wouldn't you need some serious therapy?"

"Of course therapy can be very helpful in dealing with past trauma, but if it's not accompanied by body work it is not going to be nearly as effective. You are much more than your brain, Josh, even more than your body. But it is a reality that your body experiences emotion along with your brain. Our language is littered with examples of this connection. When one is nervous, we say your "stomach is in knots." Or think of the wealth of emotion that one's can heart feel, from the light tingling of love to the heavy sadness of grief. If you listen to your body and are truly present to feel what it physically experiences, you will become more and more aware of this connection. Even if you were to look at this purely from the perspective of medical science, when emotion is experienced floods of hormones are released within the brain by the hypothalamus into the blood stream. There, they have numerous knock on effects with other organs and systems within our bodies."

"I guess I'll just have to take your word for it then," Josh replied, still obviously unconvinced.

"I understand your skepticism, Josh. Everything we have discussed thus far is merely words. Without the requisite experience to link to them they are all just concepts in your brain for you to accept or reject. Your time on this retreat is about the cultivation of personal awareness and spiritual experience so you can find these things out for yourself."

These words suddenly released the burden of analysis from Josh. He no longer felt he had to judge what has been said as his upcoming experiences would distil any truth from fiction. His body and mind experienced a wave of relaxation as he let go.

"Good." Stephanie commented. "This is the state of mind you should bring to your practices here. Simple, open awareness of the present. Don't be concerned with what is to come, or what has gone before. Just be aware of the present and everything else will take care of itself."

She handed him a printed itinerary for the rest of his stay. "Don't try and do too much," she said, "and good luck!" They both stood up with Stephanie embracing him tenderly.

"My door is always open, Josh, if you need to talk. I hope you find what you are looking for."

"Thank you," Josh replied as he began to walk toward the door, "I really appreciate that."

Josh left the office and walked out into the surrounding garden. The bright sun shone down on him, warming his face. The green vegetation surrounding him took on a luminous glow. He lay down on a patch of grass and gazed up at the clouds above him. The graceful movement of white against blue exhibited a beauty he hadn't noticed since he was a child.

He was fully absorbed in the surrounding scene, his chattering mind seemed like a distant voice of no concern to him. A smile came over his face as he lay at one with the present. His eyes slowly closed and he drifted into a deep peaceful sleep.

He was the happiest he had been since his accident, although his mind was no longer there to take note.

chapter 6

Over the next two weeks Josh immersed himself in the life of the retreat. His initial period of detox was extremely trying, with Josh left inundated with fluctuating emotions for days. The turmoil he experienced seemed to be exacerbated by his daily colonic and massage, the emotional release predicted by Stephanie a constant occurrence. At times Josh felt like he was losing his mind, one moment feeling devastatingly depressed for no reason and, in the next, awash with feelings of joyful exuberance.

The only thing providing him with some solace during this process was a small voice from within, reassuring him to 'keep going'. He could feel that this difficult course was going to be beneficial enough to brave this uncomfortable period.

He did indeed pass some gargantuan noxious waste from his colon. Upon seeing some exit, he couldn't comprehend how something so large and so obviously toxic could have remained inside of him for so long without making him ill. The truth was that it had been contributing to illnesses of both his body and mind, a constant petulance that his body's defenses would struggle with always. Now that this had been expunged, Josh felt lighter and more energized than he could remember. He had lost 6 pounds and had a youthful glow that he could feel from the inside out. Being previously resigned to a pale complexion as a consequence of his lifestyle, he was amazed by the healthy color now present in his face.

The days passed quickly in his tranquil surroundings. All the luxuries of a 'normal' health spa were present, with Josh enjoying hours of immersion in mineral baths, the relaxation of guided Tai Chi classes, and a daily helping of meditation. Having never previously attempted it before, he was constantly concerned with what he had to 'do'.

"Just concentrate on your breath..."

"...feel the sensation of air move through your nose and into your lungs..."

"...count from one to ten and don't let your mind wander. As soon as it does, start again at one..."

These were some of the suggestions proffered by his meditation instructors. "Don't let your mind wander!" Josh thought. It seemed that that was all his mind was capable of doing! This belief was explicitly highlighted every time he tried to meditate. His normal stream of thoughts provided the background noise of his daily waking life, so ubiquitous that he had not even realized they were there. This was until he was told to try and shut them off, with their monotonous drone seeming to magnify into a powerful roar.

The added attention brought to bear on his frenetic mind was both the source of his success and the reason behind his continued disappointment with his practice. His constant thought stream reduced considerably each time he sat down on his zafu, with the river of hundreds of thoughts slowing down to the trickle of a handful. Feelings of failure of having these random thoughts could have been substituted with the idea of success, success that he noticed that he was having them! However, despite these misgivings, he continued to do as he was told and practiced diligently, with positive consequences present and growing, even if they were not immediately noticed.

Throughout his stay he searched for anyone who remembered meeting or may have known of Zach. This pursuit proved to be the least satisfying part of his visit, with all enquiries appearing fruitless. He comforted himself with the knowledge that he hadn't been there that long and that someone would surely turn up soon with the information he needed. This story worked for a time but as the days continued to pass without result he found it increasingly difficult to keep the faith.

After two weeks, with his time at the retreat drawing to a close, Josh realized he was petrified. He was so emotionally invested in finding Zach that he hadn't allowed the thought that he wouldn't enter his mind until that moment.

What would he do? Any consideration of returning to his old life was still unpalatable, completely unacceptable. He was no longer that person and could never be so again. It was as if he was trying to pick up his life at the point he left it 10 years ago. He feared if he was unable to perform this miraculous act of temporal displacement he would be permanently adrift in the world, left in the mire of a vacuous existence.

He hopelessly tried to rationalize with himself, "You own your own company, you're young, have loads of money, respect, most people would kill for your life..."

Despite the recognition of these truisms, such deliberation bought him no solace. The promise of happiness in the consumer paradise that he had fought hard for and won was nothing but a hollow shell, a void that could never be filled with any temporary sedation. All his illusions were permanently removed by the twisted fuselage of flight 91.

One activity that Josh had taken to surprisingly during his stay was yoga. The system of guided stretching resonated strongly with him. His 'monkey mind' would become quiet as he entered the yoga studio in anticipation of the imminent activity. He had previously loved going to the gym and working out. He had found great pleasure in pushing exceedingly heavy weights and developing his strength. He now came to realize that his real motivation lay in the brief periods of calm from his usual mental chatter, all generated by a focus on the immediate task of pumping iron.

Even with this strength he had cultivated, he still found some yoga poses difficult to hold for any length of time. Struggling to suppress involuntary groans as beads of sweat gathered on his forehead, he was repeatedly baffled with some of the slender females in his class, all holding the same contorted position effortlessly. Any bruising his ego received by this display was minor compared to the marvelous feeling of body unity he felt during and after the class. This feeling ensured his return at least once a day.

After rising from the corpse pose at the completion of one such class, everyone sat down cross legged as they awaited some final words from their instructor.

"That was a great effort everyone. We were concentrating on releasing the neck area today so you should feel very relaxed and free through the neck and head. If you don't, that means you were holding tension while in the poses and trying to force the stretch. Yoga is one form of exercise where you should walk away feeling relaxed and energized after completing a workout, unlike most modern exercise routines where you are obviously tired and depleted. I hope you can all appreciate that with how you are feeling now, and enjoy the rest of your day. Thank you."

She placed her hands in prayer position in front of her heart, bowed her head and said, "Namaste". The class responded with the same in unison and returned the salutation.

As Josh and his classmates began rolling up their yoga mats, the instructor turned to them again, "Sorry everyone, I almost forgot. We have a visiting yoga instructor joining us later today to give an introductory class in Kundalini yoga. It will begin here at five o'clock and you're all invited to attend."

With that, she turned and was gone from the studio. Josh's new found passion for yoga made him a guaranteed participant, immediately deciding to forgo his conflicting massage appointment.

After a short nap and soak in a mineral bath, five o'clock came around quickly. He soon found himself back in the yoga studio, this time with many more people than usual. The walls had some new information posters affixed to them, with most depicting a serpent rising up the spine of their subject in various forms. The anticipation was palpable in the room, making Josh feel uneasy considering that this was only yoga. He began to consider leaving when the guest instructor came bursting into the room and closed his only exit.

"Good afternoon everyone," she commenced, looking around the room with lively eyes, "my name is Prama Chakyar."

Prama was a 50 year old woman whom exuded a powerful aura that touched everyone in the room, despite her short stature of just over five foot. She entered the studio wearing lavish purple robes draped with long necklaces. After greeting the class she proceeded to remove her outer garments to reveal tight black three quarter length pants and a fitted emerald singlet top. The disparity from what Josh took to be traditional Indian dress to what a young aerobics instructor would sport left any expectations he had unstable at best. This was reinforced by her body being more fitting on a 20 year old than an older revered yoga instructor, causing Josh's mind to unconsciously shift from perceiving her solely as an educator to a sexual being.

Prama unrolled her well-worn mat, sat down at the front of the class in the full lotus position and slowly turned her head, scanning the faces of the class with a knowing smile. The class looked on in silence.

"Welcome," she said, "to Kundalini yoga. First, a word of warning for you all. If you choose to embark down the path of studying Kundalini yoga you may find yourself and your perception of the world forever changed. I am not talking about a change you may experience from a change in belief, an increase in knowledge or indeed greater flexibility – although all of these will probably occur. What I am talking about is a change on the cellular level of your being. If you are to reach the goal of Kundalini yoga you will cease to be the person that you are now and be reborn into something else…"

Josh squirmed in his cross legged position as a wave of skepticism descended over him. A few other class members were experiencing similar emotions after the word 'reborn' was uttered, the negative religious connotations of the word linked to images of crazed evangelicals.

Josh caught himself in the chase of negative thoughts and brought himself back to the present moment with a couple of deep breaths.

"Wow!" he thought. "Well done, you are getting much better at this!" congratulating himself for his presence of mind. This praise quickly led to another distracting flurry of thoughts, again having to draw himself back to his surroundings by focusing on his breath.

"The goal of Kundalini yoga," she continued, "is the same as the goal for all forms of yoga - to coax the body into a state of Kundalini awakening. I realize that this is not a commonly stated goal, especially now as many yoga instructors have divorced all spiritual connection with their discipline. The yoga of today has too often been reduced to a series of stretches and breathing to some new age music."

She turned her head as a twinge of sadness manifested in her eyes.

"A sad price that has been paid for its proliferation throughout the west."

Her mood noticeably shifted again as she flashed a sneaky smile at the class, "So… little do many practitioners know the deep spiritual forces that are at play when they perform their morning routine!"

A tall brunette woman with wise emerald eyes raised her hand to speak. "But surely with the spread of a 'watered-down' yoga, one who truly connects with it will be inspired to seek out the deeper meaning behind their weekly class?"

"True, very true," Prama nodded. "Indeed, I am sure that this is what has brought a number of you to this retreat and to this very point in time and space."

Prama stood and began to pace across the room in front of the class, her hands clasped behind her, continuing to speak.

"The purpose of yoga is to awaken a dormant evolutionary force located at the base of our spine. This is depicted in ancient texts and illustrations as a snake or serpent, coiled three and a half times, sleeping, waiting to be awakened. When unleashed, this serpent force slithers up our spine and into our brain, lifting our consciousness to a higher level. The key to this process is the sublimation of sexual energies within us, redirected from outward reproduction to inner transformation."

Josh put up his hand, "But we don't have any control over the reproductive process other than the choice to have sex.

The whole process of the creation of life is largely unconscious."

"As is the process of sex for many people," Prama added, laughing. "You are right, the sexual experience is a haze of feeling and emotion for most people that culminates in a blissful moment of ego loss... if you're lucky." She winked again. "However, this doesn't negate the fact that there are a myriad of energetic processes involved. Awareness of these can be cultivated and with awareness comes a great deal of conscious control. As with everything, without awareness, you are merely a passenger to a series of unconscious instincts and habits that run your life."

She stopped walking and turned to face the class in the center of the room. "Thus, the sexual act can be used for spiritual cultivation, as it is in various tantric and Taoist traditions."

A boisterous voice shouted from the back of the room, "I like the sound of that!" followed by a chuckle that spread amongst the audience.

Prama smiled and continued.

"However... in Kundalini yoga, we are working with the same energies in a non-aroused state. This same force that gives birth to the creation of life, when unleashed internally within us, brings about a major transformation of body, mind and spirit. Like night and day, one is never the same person again after a Kundalini awakening."

A shapely woman from the back of the class raised her hand, "So what does stretching have to do with using our sexual energy?"

"An excellent question. Firstly, I assume you are referring to yoga when you ask about stretching. Yoga is a science of the integration of body and mind, of opening and cleansing the 72,000 nadis, or energy channels, throughout the body. All of the different poses of yoga are designed to energize and clear these energy channels, in combination with pranayama or breath control, so that your body's prana can flow freely. The flexibility you gain is a side effect of this process, a sign of the inner work being performed on your inner energetic body. Although as I mentioned before, stretching has become the unfortunate focus in some yoga classes."

A fit, elderly man sitting in the back of the room raised his hand with a question. "How important is the focus on your breath? I go to some yoga classes where it is barely mentioned, and others where it is emphasized above everything else?"

"Thank you for your question. A very important topic," Prama mused. "In a way, both teachers speak the truth but what applies to whom depends on the student's level of development. First, you must concentrate your attention on the perfection of the asanas, or body postures. If one tries to integrate breath control when one hasn't developed sufficient range of motion in their postures, breathing will be shallow and the posture will be compromised. However, when one has reached a level of confidence with their asanas the breath must be considered. Pranayama is comprised of three aspects; inhalation, exhalation and retention of breath. Through its practice, the flow of prana is regulated in the nadis of the body, as well as regulating the practitioner's thoughts and actions. It is only through the correct application of pranayama that one can cultivate the willpower needed to commit to the long, difficult path that leads to a spiritual awakening."

Another slender arm was raised from the crowd to ask a question.

"So how does that relate to Kundalini yoga?"

"Kundalini yoga specifically concentrates on working the body's three main nadis, the Ida, Pingala and Shushumna. These are the three large channels that run up the center of the body, connecting the base of the spine with the head, and tying together all of the major chakra centers. The Ida represents cool lunar energy of negative polarity and is pale in color. The Pingala is its opposite, representing hot solar energy of positive polarity and is red in color. These both coil around the central channel of Shushumna – the main conduit for Kundalini energy. Through the various poses of Kundalini yoga, many concentrating around the spine for obvious reasons, these side channels are stimulated and cleansed in order to initiate the commencement of a Kundalini awakening."

"So, are we trying to bring about enlightenment?" asked another class member.

"Mmmm..." hummed Prama, contemplating her answer.

"The term enlightenment is one that is heavily loaded with one's personal religious proclivities. Personally, I believe it's something akin to enlightenment. I would go so far as to say that all the great saints and sages throughout history have all had some form of Kundalini awakening that has helped imbue them with their spiritual authority. The different 'symptoms' of a Kundalini awakening can be found in personal reflections of people from many different religious and cultural traditions. For example, the famous psychologist Carl Jung describes such a personal experience in his writings and then seeks to define it within his concept of individuation.

He was a man who became fascinated with the teachings and processes of a Kundalini awakening and other similar esoteric traditions, believing them to hold the keys to our own psychological salvation."

Prama sat back down in the full lotus position on her mat in front of the class and let out a deep sigh. "Unfortunately, like so much in life, everything I have said is just words. I hope I have fed your intellectual curiosity a bit with my introduction, to motivate you to seek and practice more, because in the end, practice and experience are the only things that are going to give any of my words true meaning for you."

With these final statements, Prama began leading the class through a series of yoga postures.

Externally, Josh couldn't see much difference between these yoga poses and the ones that he had been learning before, other than the emphasis on the spine as Prama had previously stated. Despite this, he felt a different intention to the practice now from the group, one of a solemn spiritual discipline that was not there before. There was a pervasive feeling that the class was now doing something greater than themselves, all participating in an activity held in great reverence which each participant feeling honored to have been included.

After one and a half hours of practice, the class finally came to an end with the chime of a bell.

"I thank you all for sharing your beautiful practice with me today and wish you well on the path that is the spiritual landscape of your lives." She placed her hands in the prayer position and bowed her head.

"Namaste."

The class again mimicked her actions and returned the reverent word.

Everyone filed out of the room silently, each trying to capture some of the sacred space created within the room to carry back into the world outside. Josh felt exuberant as he always did after a yoga session but was intrigued by the increased importance Prama seemed to place on her discipline. He delayed packing up his things until the last class member had left and then approached his new instructor. She was bent over her mat, rolling it up preparing for her own departure.

"Excuse me, may I ask you a couple of questions about the class?"

She turned around and stood up. "Of course, how can I help you..."

"Josh. Josh Black."

She offered her hand, which Josh quickly took.

"A pleasure to meet you Josh. Thank you so much for participating in my class. I hope that you received something of value."

"I always do from yoga," he replied. "But I have never heard yoga spoken of as you did today. Frankly, I am still quite skeptical about the existence of the so called 'energy' everyone seems to be captivated by at this place. Sure, the beauty of this place and the activities here help people relax and de-stress, but all this talk of 'mystical forces' frankly makes my skin crawl."

"Josh, one of the many paradoxes of life is that we both shape and create our reality by the beliefs that we hold, and yet, there clearly is some form of objective reality that exists, irrespective of our beliefs. For example, for a time the ancient Greeks believed that the veins that travel throughout our body were empty tubes. Do you think their lack of 'belief' in blood flowing through their veins made the blood flow any less?"

"So you are comparing my scientific view of the world with the pre-science of Ancient Greece?" he retorted defensively.

"The views of current science are closer to the beliefs I hold than you may think Josh."

"There is no concept of mystical energy in science..." Josh stated.

"True, for now, but there is such a thing as bio-energy..."

"Bio-energy?" Josh asked.

"Yes. It has been shown that the body operates like a large electric circuit. Electric currents have been detected in many shapes and forms throughout the body, all vital to its functioning. Take the modern EEG machine, the electroencephalograph for monitoring the brain, or the ECG, the electrocardiograph for monitoring the heart – both devices measure different areas of electrical activity of the body."

"But that is something easily measurable. What you are talking about is not."

"Again, not yet. Would you say the location of acupuncture points is easily measurable?

Acupuncture is a system of medicine that stimulates points that directly influence the body's internal energy levels to improve health and wellbeing."

"Of course they can't!"

"And there you would be wrong Josh. Science has found a surprising correlation between areas of increased skin conductivity and the acupuncture points traditionally prescribed in Chinese medicine."

Caught off guard by this new information, Josh began to backtrack.

"Look, I'm sure there is something to these different ancient practices. Otherwise, I wouldn't feel the way I do after practicing. I'm just saying that I find it a little hard to believe the depth of the claims about the mystical many make."

"Okay then, how about the chakras? Do you think that they are real?"

"To be honest, not really. I have never felt anything like you and others have described and certainly can't see anything as some claim to be able to."

"More practice, Josh. That is all you require and your sensitivity would be heightened. Close your eyes for a moment please."

Josh hesitated for a moment, staring back at Prama wondering what she was planning to do. Seeing there was no reason not to trust her, he decided to oblige the request, temporarily closing off his external visual world. He could immediately feel a slight flow of air, corresponding to some movements that Prama was performing with her hands. He tried to keep his mind present and relaxed.

Josh began to feel a faint tingling sensation in his chest, drawing his focus. Upon noticing this feeling, it increased in intensity, with an accompanying sensation of heat. As it was quite pleasurable, Josh kept focusing on it, losing himself in the sensation. His focus helped the feeling to intensify further, transforming into a concentrated sphere of warm energy rotating in the area of his solar plexus.

No questions arose in his mind as to what was happening. Josh simply surrendered to the sensation. He began to feel waves of heat moving through his entire body, pulsating from this radiant center. His breathing rate and depth steadily increased as the passage of heat became more intense. A sense of euphoria accompanied the waves, with his body beginning to rock back and forth. Josh's mouth opened into a wide smile.

Suddenly, a feeling of immense sadness arose deep within his lungs, spilling out and washing over him. Totally open and unprepared, Josh started to cry uncontrollably, with tears quickly streaming down his cheeks.

The sadness was overwhelming but strangely cleansing, his mind feeling lighter as the emotion travelled through him. Josh opened his eyes and found himself curled up on the ground wrapped in Prama's arms.

Neither spoke for some minutes, with Prama gently rubbing his back. When the flood of tears finally abated, Josh removed himself from her embrace.

"What... did you just do to me?" Josh asked, wiping away the moisture from his cheeks.

"I'm sorry, I didn't expect you to have such an intense release. You obviously have a lot of emotional turmoil locked up within your body that you haven't yet expressed."

"But what did you DO?" Josh cried in exasperation.

"I gave you a burst of prana, to help open up your blocked solar plexus chakra."

"Ah, now that makes total sense," Josh said sarcastically, wiping his eyes and trying to compose himself.

"Josh, I can see and feel that you have lost your connection with the surrounding world, with the universe that is your home. I figure that this is what has brought you to the Enso center in the first place."

Josh sat in silence, managing a small nod of acknowledgement.

"The solar plexus chakra is concerned with this feeling of interconnectedness, of being grounded in your place in the world. Part of the reason you have lost this connection is due to a major energetic blockage in this chakra. This would cause this feeling of disconnection, also prompting you to withdraw from emotional investment in relationships. This can even manifest as far as divorcing love from sexual experience, as the solar plexus acts as a bridge between the heart chakra and the sacral chakra, associated with one's sexuality."

"But why was I overcome with this incredible sadness then?" Josh asked. "But I did first feel an amazing sensation. I almost felt free of myself but a part of everything."

He paused for a moment, considering what he had just said.

"...if that makes any sense," Josh added, slightly embarrassed by his statement.

"Yes, Josh, it does. If you can imagine the energy channels of the body as water pipes, I merely applied a pressure hose to a blocked opening, helping flush away some constrictive refuse. As the energy spilled out from your center and filtered throughout your body this helped dislodge some other deeply held psychic trauma. It seemed to come from your lungs where you have been holding some profound grief. This resulted in the cathartic experience you had. I'm sorry but I feel that you still have a long way to go to heal this trauma, but what you experienced with me today is a good start."

With every truthful revelation Prama made, Josh fell into a deeper state of confusion. He had indeed just had a firsthand esoteric experience, with this seeming to confirm the truth of a number of spiritual terms that were still intellectually nonsensical to him. This, followed with a vivid description of his own psychic malaise from someone he had just met, further confused any rational understanding he had of the world around him. Talk of the calming properties of meditation, or the healing possibilities of detoxification programs involving diet and colonics seemed to occupy the bedrock of common sense compared to what he was now being presented to accept as reality.

Reflecting back on Doctor Oberson's warning of the trauma involved in an involuntary switch to a spiritual paradigm, in this moment his statement could not have been more apt.

Exasperated, he let out a loud torrent of air from his lungs. "I am literally speechless, Prama. How in the hell am I supposed to make sense of this? How can you?"

"I have been exposed to these ideas and feelings for most of my life, so I can't see how they don't make sense. I'd find it impossible to perceive the world in any other way."

Prama looked into Josh's eyes, sensing the terror of a frightened child.

"But I know that this does not help you. I can only imagine how traumatic these realizations must be when forced upon an unsuspecting psyche. The spiritual path is not without substantial difficulties, things sent to test us on our journey. Our very sanity can be tested when focusing on and unleashing the dormant evolutionary forces that lie within us. Without the proper instruction one can indeed become lost."

She reached over and placed her hand on his cheek, rubbing it gently.

"But that is not the case here, Josh. You are surrounded by a supportive spiritual community, all concerned with your wellbeing. You are not alone, Josh. You have made great progress here today and throughout your stay here. You have come a very long way in a very short time."

Josh's breathing became deep and relaxed as he took in the sound of her words and the touch of her hand. He began to see a faint shimmering light surrounding her head as his feelings of confusion fell away from his body and mind.

"All the things that you knew about your body before are still true. Your heart still pumps blood to feed your body with oxygen and nutrients, your brain still allows a place for your thoughts to manifest in this world. You will gradually integrate all that you have learned into a greater vision of yourself and the world around you. Your chakras that you have begun to viscerally experience today all influence your physical form. They all have an acute physical relationship with the hormone and nerve centers of your body, helping to physically regulate your body and mind, in addition to their greater energetic relationship to your larger spiritual self."

Prama took her hand away from Josh's face and placed it in her lap. Calm had returned to Josh with his analytical mind again eager to comprehend what she had just said.

"How are they related to the hormones?"

Prama smiled with the return of inquisitive Josh.

"Each of the major seven chakra centers has a direct relationship to the body's endocrine system."

"Which produces hormones?" Josh asked.

"Right," Prama confirmed. "The endocrine glands have a vital function in maintaining homeostasis in the body, regulating growth and development and mobilizing the body's immune system. It is similar to the nervous system in being a messenger service of the body, the difference being that it is made up of chemical rather than electrical signals and consequently acts much more slowly over time than the instantaneous response of a nerve cell firing. However, there is still some contention about which glands are paired with which chakras."

She stood up and walked over to a colorful wall chart. It depicted a man seated in the full lotus position with intricately detailed depictions of the seven major chakras placed over his central axis. She moved her finger to the base of the man's spine.

"For example, the root chakra, or Muladhara, is related to the amount of raw physical energy one enjoys, our survival needs, and one's will to live.

Many people hold it to be paired with the adrenal glands on top of the kidneys. This is partly due to their function in our survival, with the adrenals responsible for the 'fight or flight' response when we are in danger. But others hold the sexual organs to be the appropriate paired system, with our strength and vitality intimately associated with our sexual virility. The serpent of Kundalini is often depicted as a snake coiled three and a half times around itself in this position. Here it lies dormant, awaiting its call to rise."

"If there is all this disagreement among people, how can you really be sure that there are any links?" Josh asked.

"This kind of discussion is healthy, as long as one realizes that we are standing at the beginning of a long process. I have friends who will debate these issues for hours, each holding steadfastly to their beliefs formed through both spiritual experience and academic research. I listen with interest and occasionally play devil's advocate but I don't have any firm views. We really are in our infancy in making these connections but I have no doubt that they exist."

"But how do you know?"

"Through my own experience and research. No one believes that the chakras exist as these highly stylized, symbolic representations that you see here. These merely provide a window in which we can access their transformative energy. Some people don't even need this education, instead having a spontaneous Kundalini awakening as I discussed with the class. If you read some of the accounts of Gopi Krishna and his experience with Kundalini energy, I think we can begin to appreciate the raw process of physiological transformation that takes place through this. He describes how the energy of his sexual organs was redirected within himself, constantly pumping a powerful, magnificent force up his spine, throughout his body, and bathing his brain. After barely surviving the various trials and traumas he initially experienced through this process, he was left as a man totally transformed, with his perception of the world transformed along with him."

"So you think it is only a matter of time until we have some physical evidence of all of this?" Josh asked.

"Our knowledge of the endocrine and nervous system is constantly expanding, as is the vast majority of medical knowledge today. New questions are being raised all the time, and many things that we once believed impossible are being rewritten through the scientific study of realized spiritual practitioners.

I firmly believe that if the scientific community opens its heart and mind, expands the perceived possibilities of the human body from being a mere biochemical machine to a spiritual vehicle, these tenuous connections of today will be expanded into knowledge that will usher in a new dawn for humanity. You have had a taste of these possibilities here today Josh. You haven't been told about it, you haven't studied it, you have experienced it. Personal spiritual experience is the key. The key to everything. Through these spiritual experiences, one can change oneself and help change the world."

Josh could only sit and listen. He couldn't dispute her logic. He had indeed experienced something profound and he couldn't deny it. But he was still scared. His experiences were so foreign to him and had powerful consequences that he still could not even begin to understand. He could only judge them based on his experience. And his experience had brought both elation and crushing grief.

He looked up at her and stammered.

"But… I'm still scared… Why am I so scared?"

"Fear is normal, Josh. Fear of the unknown is an ancient evolutionary survival mechanism, designed to keep us safe. But it is this same fear, when not faced and conquered, that can lead to all the ugliness that the human race continues to deal with. Racism, religious violence and war all have their roots in this fear. Acknowledge your fear Josh, follow your heart and keep going."

Josh's eyes darted across the room and he pursed his lips, betraying the cynicism he felt. Pondering her last statement and anticipating this possible reaction from Josh's usually skeptical mind, Prama added:

"Clichés often become so for a reason, Josh. They can embody universal truths that must be said again and again to deeply permeate the collective consciousness. Trust you are on a wonderful journey and know everything is perfect."

Prama helped him up and gave him a warm embrace. She released him and placed her hands in prayer position in front of her heart and bowed.

"Namaste," Prama said.

Josh again reciprocated her gesture of respect.

"Namaste. And thank you so much." Josh replied.

He slowly walked over to the door and grasped the brass handle, slowly turning it. As he pushed opened the heavy wooden door, he realized that he had forgotten the very question that he remained behind class to ask. He turned back to Prama.

"I'm sorry, Prama, excuse me again." he started.

"Yes?" Prama asked, draping her purple robes over her shoulders once more.

"Do you remember meeting an old student here by the name of Zach Holtzman?" Josh asked.

Prama looked at him and smiled. "Yes, I do, Josh."

chapter 7

Three days after his conversation with Prama, Josh found himself exiting Dalian Zhoushuizi International Airport in Liaoning province, China. Prama told Josh how she had taught Zach for a time during his extended stay at the Enso retreat. Ever the inquisitive student, Zach was fascinated by the promise of a Kundalini awakening, training diligently with Prama every chance he had.

Enchanted by the mysterious energy he could now feel coursing through his body, Zach was ravenous for knowledge, devouring every book he could find at the center related to the subject. During one of many discussions Zach had initiated after class, Prama mentioned studies she had undertaken with an eminent Chinese medical practitioner that helped her better understand her own unfolding spiritual reality.

Having relentlessly probed every instructor at the retreat for spiritual insight, the vision of such an untapped wealth of information proved irresistible to Zach. He pleaded with Prama for a formal introduction and through his tenacious enthusiasm was accepted as an apprentice, moving to China soon after.

Finally equipped with the knowledge to continue his search, Josh felt a growing anxiety as he prepared to leave the sanctuary of the retreat. He had grown pleasantly accustomed to the beautiful surroundings and serene population of people whom he had shared his time with. He wanted to imbue his being with the tranquil essence that surrounded him in his final days, but was always left with the same question… how would one go about doing that?

With the burden of finding someone who had known Zach released, Josh found he was finally able to really let go and savor his experience. His remaining days were not enough. He felt like he could have easily stayed on happily as a permanent guest. Despite such idle musings, he knew that he couldn't allow this to happen.

He knew that his quest remained to be fulfilled.

Escape from his new destiny lay neither in burying himself in work like he had done before or in retreating into his current idyllic surroundings. Both options were equally detached from the world around him. Contemplating this, Josh began to realize that the beauty that we find in life is often rooted in its impermanence.

In Josh's final meeting with his retreat coordinator, Stephanie, she warned him of the disorientating effects that he could experience when re-joining the 'real world' again. A long stay outside the normal daily corporate assault we experience was akin to immersion in a sensory deprivation tank of sorts. Being bathed daily in the beauty of the natural world and living amongst architecture designed to bring about a harmonious state of mind can sit in stark contrast to the brash, often unforgiving spaces of our concrete mega cities. With stimulation flooding in from all directions, the cacophony of sights and sounds can easily leave one in a state of permanent distraction.

This everyday experience is amplified when one has been removed from its grasp for a time. As he journeyed from the Enso retreat to China, Josh could feel his head spinning as he tried to adjust to the increasing urbanization of his surroundings. Initially wondering how he ever managed to concentrate on anything with so much occurring around him, he slowly became acclimatized once again. The mind's screening ability seemed almost mystical to him, as within hours the overwhelming sights and sounds were confined to a dull rumble deep within his subconscious, again working their hidden effects on his waking life.

After hailing a taxi, Josh found himself whisked through the streets of Dalian. Often said to be China's most beautiful city, Dalian lies on the coast in North Eastern China, located in the middle of the Liaodong Peninsula. The taxi soon dropped Josh at the five star Shangri-La Hotel, located at the center of the thriving commercial district of the city. After checking in and taking a quick shower, he was soon downstairs discussing the whereabouts of the doctor he sought with the concierge. After warning him of the long, expensive taxi ride that awaited him, the concierge quickly communicated his destination to a waiting driver and Josh was on his way.

After over two hours in the car driving north-west away from the city, they had traded the rapid urbanization of Dalian for a rural China that seemed to have had time set on pause. Everywhere he looked he could see people performing backbreaking manual labor. Tasks usually requiring machine assistance today were being tackled here with sheer human force.

He saw a large building being demolished by a swarm of busy laborers, with not a single wrecking ball in sight. They all moved quickly to dispose of the pieces they had reefed from the structural relic, only to quickly return for more.

The taxi travelled by a small village and entered a grove of bamboo. As they curved around a bend in the road the driver started to speak, slowing down and gesturing out the side window. Josh could see that they had arrived.

After paying his driver, Josh stepped out of the car. He stood in front of a simple white building with a flat roof. No windows were exposed to the street, with the only entrance blocked by a line of people spilling out of the building. Most of them seemed to be in small groups, with many carrying bags of food and other random trinkets. Some seemed to be terminally ill, their haggard faces and emaciated bodies giving the impression that they did not have long for left in this world.

Unaware of the protocols that he should follow, Josh went and joined the back of the queue. As he walked over, a myriad of eyes followed his movements. An able bodied Caucasian was a unique sight to most at this location. Despite this anomaly, interest in him was soon lost, as all were more concerned with the ailments that had brought them there than some strange white pilgrim.

After waiting for half an hour and still unable to see inside the building, Josh was becoming impatient. His lack of language skills left him feeling impotent, unable to communicate to anyone in their native tongue and find out what was going on. He decided to revert to the all too familiar catch cry of the western traveler.

"Does anyone here speak English?" he asked the people in the line in front of him. Heads all turned in unison towards him, and then to each other, all commenting on the disruptive foreigner.

"Anyone?" he tried again exasperated. Despondent, he wondered how he would even begin to communicate with the doctor himself if he ever got to see him. With his head down staring at his shoes he heard an intelligible voice.

"You alright?" a voice beckoned. It belonged to a round smiling face of Chinese extraction, sticking out the corner of the doorway. Josh was caught off guard.

"Yes... umm... I'm here to see Doctor Shen."

"Yes!" the man responded, throwing his arms in the air. "So is everybody!"

"Sorry. Yes. I mean, I'm not sick, I just need to speak to him for a moment. When do you think he'll be free?"

"Closing time at eight. Maybe you can speak to him then?"

"Great!" Josh said, relieved. "Thanks for your help."

He exited the queue and visibly relaxed. Having a personal aversion to standing idly in lines for long periods, he had allowed significant tension to build inside him. With that released, he was now free to spend his time exploring for a few hours. Returning at just after eight, he was relieved to see the line of people no longer present. He knocked on the door three times and waited.

Some Chinese words were spoken behind the door as it slowly edged open. He was greeted by a young Chinese man in a white coat.

"Doctor Shen?" Josh enquired.

The man rolled his eyes and turned around, walking back into the building yelling, "Foon!"

Hearing the quick shuffle of footsteps from within, he was again greeted with the same friendly, English speaking face from earlier.

"Yes?" he asked.

"Hi. You remember me from before? I'm here to see Doctor Shen."

"Of course!" he smiled. "Doctor Shen is not here."

"But you said he would finish at eight o'clock?" Josh said.

"Yes, I did, and now it is eight fifteen. Clinic opens at eight o'clock tomorrow morning. He will be back then. See you!"

"But what do..."

The door shut with a thud, cutting his question short.

Cursing under his breath, Josh made his way back to the small village nearby. Not keen for the extended taxi ride back into Dalian, he had noticed a modest inn earlier in the day that would have to do in providing shelter for the night.

After mustering some robotic tones from his electronic dictionary, a little creative sign language and the exchange of Chinese currency, he secured a small room and settled in for an early night.

Determined to catch the doctor first thing and not repeat the events of the previous day, Josh set off early, arriving at the clinic at a quarter to eight. With the clinic entrance in sight, he was relieved to see the door already open and no line extending out the door. He bounded up to the door and entered the building.

He was greeted with an average sized room that looked in need of some maintenance. Paint peeled off the walls in sections, with cracks forming in all four corners of the ceiling. Framed, sun bleached charts adorned one wall, all depicting the acupuncture points and energetic meridians of the body from various viewpoints.

A comprehensive herbal dispensary sat at the back of the room, the wall lined with an impressive array of small wooden drawers that stretched from the floor to the ceiling. An assistant stood on a small metal step ladder placed near the left wall, allowing him access to the upper shelves. A large wooden table sat between the shelves and the rest of the room, with some antique golden measuring scales sitting to one side.

The remaining edges of the room were lined with rows of seats. He was dismayed to find the majority of these were already filled with patients. A number of people in white coats darted around the room attending to various tasks, with the round faced English speaker from the day before nowhere to be seen. Figuring that the only way to guarantee an audience with Doctor Shen was to join the line of patients, he sat down, finding some comfort that this wait would at least be seated.

Patients filed in and out as Josh's turn gradually drew closer. Most patients were again brandishing some kind of gift for the doctor, something he scolded himself for overlooking a second time. People exiting the treatment room had expressions of immense relief on their faces, with most carrying a herbal prescription to the dispensary for one of the many apprentices to fill.

With the sun beginning to approach its zenith for the day, Josh was finally directed by an apprentice to go into the treatment room. Parting the curtains separating those waiting from those being treated, Josh saw a similar sized room filled to capacity with treatment tables. Narrow aisles crisscrossed the room, allowing access to each patient from all sides by the doctor.

The majority of beds were filled with the infirm who all had acupuncture needles penetrating into points specific for each condition.

He saw the doctor working on a particular patient and quietly approached, waiting for him to finish.

Doctor Shen Fei-Hung stood at just over five feet tall. He had a full head of hair, small angular face and a slight frame. He was wearing plain black pants, simple black leather shoes and a white doctor's coat. He had a face that would easily blend into a crowd but his eyes revealed something more.

The doctor lent over the woman's leg he was treating and twirled the acupuncture needle back and forth. The hairs on the back of Josh's neck stood up as he lent closer to observe. The air seemed charged, as though lighting could abruptly burst forth from the ceiling at any moment. Without warning, the patient's leg began to twitch. As if passing an electrical current from his hand through the needle, the spasm increased, resulting in a pulsating muscle contraction. Josh looked up at the patient. She lay there with her lips wearing a serene smile and her eyes gently closed. The doctor continued to manipulate the needle with the patient's leg still twitching involuntarily.

"Wow..." Josh whispered.

The atmosphere of the room suddenly shifted again as the doctor stopped treating the patient and turned to look back at Josh.

"Yes?" he asked.

"Uhhh..." Josh stammered. "Sorry for interrupting, Doctor, I just wanted to ask you a couple of questions."

"Are you sick?"

"...Umm, no, I just..."

"Look at all these people." The doctor motioned around the room.

"Some have travelled for hours, many walked with injured limbs. I can't make them wait with your idle chatter."

Doctor Shen then turned around and continued treating his patient.

"May I speak to you after you have finished treating them?" Josh asked quietly.

"It's your life. You are welcome to wait."

With his head down, Josh turned around and walked back to the waiting room, dragging his feet like a petulant child as he left. "Just a couple of questions…" he thought, dreading the upcoming wait he would have to endure.

Due to the early hour, he still managed to find an empty seat. Claiming one, he sat down and let out a deep sigh as his wait commenced. He again looked around the room. Different people from yesterday filled the seats, but their maladies seemed all too familiar.

Time had left its undeniable mark on many; what once was supple, now was stiff, what once was toned, now lay flaccid. Some were nursing broken bones, others had external lacerations that were bandaged but still leaking blood. A kaleidoscope of facial complexions surrounded him, changing from fiery red to dull yellow, pasty grey to deathly blue. Looking around the room pondering the suffering before him, he was disgusted with himself.

He was upset over having to wait to speak to someone.

That was his problem.

His attention drifted inside his body. He was present as air filled his lungs and his heart drove blood around his body. He was in no pain; he had no illness to complain of. Indeed, he felt as good as any time he could remember in his life. With these facts present in his mind, his wait no longer seemed so arduous. He sat there patiently for the rest of the day.

Patients continued to file in and out for the entire day until the sun had set. All had left the treatment room with expressions of relief despite their particular individual ailments. After releasing his final patient, Doctor Shen removed his clinic jacket and hung it on a brass hook behind the front door. He bid a brief farewell to his apprentices and proceeded to walk out of the clinic and towards his home. Josh hurried along behind him and began to give him an account of his journey up until that moment. Doctor Shen walked on in silence with his hands clasped behind him, barely acknowledging his story.

After the exhaustive retelling, Josh was anxious for the doctor's response.

"Well….will you help me?" Josh asked.

"Mmmmm… much to consider." the doctor replied.

"Such as?"

"You have started on this quest for your friend, but you do not truly seek your friend. You seek something else. Something much more important that will help you answer the questions you have."

Doctor Shen stopped walking and faced Josh.

"Until you know what you truly seek, no one can help you."

Josh considered what he had said.

"How can I find out what I truly seek?" Josh asked.

Doctor Shen turned and continued to walk.

"No more questions for tonight. I have an idea of how I may help you but please return here at sunrise tomorrow morning. Now, I must rest – the balance of Yin and Yang requires it."

Confused by his cryptic speech but anxious for some answers, he left the doctor to return the next day.

The sun had not yet risen when he arrived the following morning, only beginning to illuminate some low lying clouds in pink hues. When he arrived Doctor Shen was already present, performing what appeared to be Tai Chi in a nearby clearing.

Josh approached him from behind, observing his graceful movements. He finished his sequence and stood motionless with closed eyes and both palms resting on his lower abdomen.

"Your friend sought me out as he wished to learn about Qi," he said. He opened his eyes, turned to face Josh and continued.

"One of the reasons you are here is for something similar."

"Why? What is Qi?" Josh asked.

"Qi has many meanings in English. Depending on the context, it could be translated as energy, breath, wind, generative force or vital energy. What I am referring to is the vital energy, the creative force that permeates all life, all existence. The root of all things, it pulses throughout your body, animating you, giving you life. When your Qi stops flowing, life has departed and your body will decay and return to the earth."

"Is this like prana in yoga?" Josh asked.

"Yes," answered Doctor Shen. "Like prana from India, Ki from Japan, many world cultures speak of this creative force that gives life. Qi is a fundamental concept to the theory and practice of Chinese Medicine. It is through the lack of Qi, or, the stagnant flow of Qi, that all disease arises."

"So this is what you treat with acupuncture?" Josh asked.

"Yes. The body is comprised of many Qi pathways, called meridians. Of these, there are 14 main meridians that run close to the surface of the body.

On these meridians lie the common acupuncture points that are used in traditional Chinese medicine clinics across the world today. That is what is represented on the charts in my waiting room. I believe you would have had a chance to look at them yesterday."

Josh nodded in acknowledgement, working to quell some residual frustration as he was reminded of his long wait.

"It is through the practice of Qi Gong that one can heal oneself. A patient can build up their own Qi and gradually dissolve blockages in their own meridians through its practice. For those who are not already ill, practicing Qi Gong can help create conditions for a long and healthy life."

"Was that what you were doing when I arrived this morning?" Josh asked.

"Yes, it was." Doctor Shen answered. "I am going to show you some beginning exercises to help you cultivate and sense Qi. With time and practice, you will be able to direct your own Qi to help you in your spiritual journey."

"You mean my journey to try and find Zach?" Josh asked.

"No. I mean the journey that is your life. First, I'm going to teach you how to breathe."

Josh laughed. "I think I know that already... I've been doing it for a few years now!"

"Once upon a time, you did know this unconsciously. But as we age, our focal point of breathing shifts and contributes to the various maladies we suffer as we age. Please, take a deep breath for me."

Josh obliged, drawing in a deep breath. Air hissed as it passed through his mouth and nose with his chest and ribcage expanding outward.

Doctor Shen walked up to Josh and placed his hand on his chest. "See. This is wrong. One's breath should not be directed here. Chest breathing is shallow. You are not allowing the air to fully fill your lungs. One must use the diaphragm and abdomen to breathe, to truly invigorate one's Qi."

He grabbed Josh's hands and placed one on his chest and one on his belly.

"Now, take a deep breath again. Only this time, do not allow the hand on your chest to move. Only move the hand on your abdomen."

Josh attempted to follow his instruction but found it surprisingly difficult. His habitual chest breathing had been unconsciously reinforced through years of repetition. Pushing out his stomach in order to fill his lungs felt awkward and unnatural.

"That doesn't feel right," Josh commented.

"All the more reason why you need to break the habit," Doctor Shen replied. "The key is not to force it. Straining your breath is counterproductive. It needs to be relaxed, which it will become over time, with practice."

"I find that hard to believe," Josh replied skeptically.

"You will be amazed how quickly your body will revert to this after only a little training. The body has an intelligence far greater than you realize. Remove the interference of the mind and allow it to find its natural rhythm again. In the art of Qi Gong, your breath is a foundational part of your practice. Everything follows from this."

He pointed just below Josh's navel.

"See this point here. It is the location of your lower dan tien. This is the primary storage point of Qi within your body. By practicing abdominal breathing, you are constantly priming this 'Qi battery' as it were. By focusing your attention on this point during meditation, you are helping to fill your dan tien with Qi. Abundance of Qi in your lower dan tien is necessary for all other Qi Gong practices, and part of the foundation for truly boundless health."

Josh stood there and practiced the breathing technique he was shown a few more times, trying to wrap his mind around what he was saying.

"Now, there is a set of moving Qi Gong exercises, distilled from the practices at the Shaolin Temple that have been taught for centuries in various forms and practiced by millions of Chinese. Called 'the Eight Pieces of Brocade', they were specifically designed to unblock each of the 12 regular meridians of the body. As the name suggests, the form is comprised of eight separate exercises, each one carefully selected to work a different group of meridians and to help invigorate different organs of the body. For many people, this is the only Qi Gong that they ever learn. But, with regular practice, it can help ward off disease and keep one's body healthy and youthful right into old age. It also lays an excellent foundation for more advanced Qi Gong practices."

Doctor Shen looked directly into Josh's eyes, focusing intently.

"Would you like to learn it?"

"Yes, thank you doctor," Josh replied.

Doctor Shen proceeded to guide Josh through the movements of the form. Correcting him as they went, they repeated each of the eight exercises a total of eight times each. The doctor moved from pose to pose with grace, his hands gliding through the air, resting momentarily to hold a position and then moving on again effortlessly. Each movement was coordinated with their breath, both slowly and deeply breathing in and out. The repetition of breath and movement worked quietly to calm the mind and encourage their Qi to move naturally. As he bent and stretched Josh could feel the beginning sensations of Qi pulsing through his body, with the feelings increasing as they proceeded through the set. Finishing, they placed their hands over their abdomens.

"Always finish any Qi Gong you are performing by bringing your focus back to your lower dan tien. This point is very important. If you don't properly store the Qi you have built through your practice, it can actually be responsible for causing disease, not preventing it."

"So Qi Gong can be dangerous?"

"Yes, if not performed correctly. You are cultivating a powerful force through its practice, the generative life force of our entire universe within the microcosm that is your human body. If one is careless in its application and does not respect this, one can do untold harm."

"I'll try and be careful," Josh said, struggling to mask his natural skepticism.

"Please do." Doctor Shen said.

Both stood and gazed at the other for a few moments. With the inevitable question now back at the forefront of Josh's mind, he spoke, carefully considering his words.

"Thank you so much Doctor Shen for teaching me about Qi Gong. I can see how such practices could help me in my life. I really do feel amazing after doing that. And I'll try and work on my breathing."

Josh paused for a moment, cautiously constructing his next sentence.

"So, now could you please tell me what you know about Zach? Do you know where he is?"

Doctor Shen pursed his lips and let out a quiet groan.

"As I said before, I believe that you are not really here to find your friend. But I will give you the information that you seek if you still want it. On one condition?"

"Which is?"

"Go back to Dalian. Find a park and practice the exercises I have shown you three times a day for the next month. After the month has passed, return to this location. If you still want the information, I will tell you what you need."

Josh reluctantly accepted Doctor Shen's proposition. After all he thought, what else was he going to do? Parting with a handshake, Doctor Shen was soon back in his clinic tending to the ill. Josh sat grinning widely in the taxi as he journeyed back to Dalian, still radiant from his guided instruction with the doctor. His mind active as always, he tried to concentrate on the health benefits he would accrue during the coming month, attempting to quell any residual impatience caused by his forced hiatus.

The month started well. He was informed by his concierge that the Dalian Botanical Gardens were located only a short walk from his hotel. With tourist map in tow he easily navigated the surrounding streets and made his way to the park. Originally founded in the early twentieth century, the expansive park was spread over 80 acres. Evergreen Cyprus and Pine varieties covered the area, with grasses and lakes all kept meticulously year round.

Upon stepping onto the grounds, Josh had a feeling of serenity descend upon him. The peaceful energy of the park sat in stark contrast to the bustling city which surrounded it. He knew at once that he had found his training ground.

He practiced for a few days with great enthusiasm, making the excursion to the particular spot that he had chosen thrice daily. It was under a magnificent Oak tree he stood, motionless at first, practicing his abdominal breathing for about twenty minutes, before moving slowly through the Eight Pieces of Brocade as instructed by Doctor Shen.

Deep within one training session, he had a direct experience of the duality of his mind. The constant stream of thoughts that were a normal part of Josh's waking life were increasingly tempered by the different techniques he had learnt, first in meditation and yoga at the Enso retreat, and now in China practicing Qi Gong. The flow of thoughts did not seem to stop, but their intensity did lessen significantly as he continued to train in his various new found disciplines.

This particular session he had his focus intently placed on his lower dan tien. He was beginning to feel the physical sensations of an energetic ball in his abdomen, something he observed with amazement. A stream of random thoughts was still present to his mind as always, but they felt more like a distant echo, happening somewhere far away. An inner dialogue arose in observation of what Josh was experiencing.

My focus is on my dan tien.

I can feel my mind here.

I can feel a ball of Qi slowly gathering...

But these other thoughts are still occurring as they normally do...

Although they seem so far away.

But then, if my focus is down here,

Who is having those thoughts up there!?

Upon thinking this, he began to lose focus on his current task. The previous background noise of his mental chatter started to increase in volume, with the energy ball beginning to dissipate. He still maintained some focus on his dan tien but that was now secondary to his habitual thought stream. Taking a deep breath, he again refocused his attention on his energetic center. The distracted mind again faded into the background, with the glow of Qi again resonating strongly in his belly. This prompted another chain of thoughts:

My usual thoughts continue on without my focus...

But then the work on my dan tien, once begun, also continued without my focus...

But I am observing both these things...

So then these processes can't be me...

So I am the observer...

Not the thoughts I am observing...

So what does that leave?

What am I!?

Rattled by his inability to answer these questions he stopped practicing, his attention quickly snapping back to focus on his surrounding world.

He sat down where he stood on the grass and looked around. Trees swayed in the distance as they were gently carried by a slight wind. People were scattered around him, all making use of the haven from the surrounding urban expanse.

Despite this picture of tranquility, difficult existential questions kept arising, continuing to unsettle him. Questions of who and what he really was spiraled round and round inside his head. He became nervous. His eyes darted from left to right, extremely agitated, knowing the unavoidable conclusion that there was no escape from one's own mind.

Old patterns of avoidance were exhumed, their previously well-oiled gears in his mind slowly creaked into action once more. What he needed was more stimulation, not less. This would occupy his mind and put him at ease. He immediately headed out of the park and into the heart of the city. The dissonant arrangement of traffic and billboards, lights and noise began the process of anesthesia he craved. He stumbled upon an appealing bar and quickly made his way inside. Before he could think otherwise, he had finished his first drink and was ordering another. Training would have to be forgone that evening.

The next morning he awoke with a nasty hangover. Rebuking himself sharply for his feeble will, he made his way to the park and went through the motions of his training. He mentally committed to not missing a session again, but inadvertently compromised his current practice by constantly thinking about not missing training again!

A couple of days later, he was caught up in a period of urban exploration and skipped his mid-day training. Lacking the concern of before, he brushed the infraction aside and still trained that evening.

With each miss a lackadaisical approach to his regime was reinforced. His lazy mind crept in. He began to sleep in. Josh became increasingly enamored with his host city's nightlife and the young women that enjoy it, causing further interruptions to his training. This behavior continued to be reinforced until only a couple of days before the end of his month. The reunion with Doctor Shen now looming, he realized that he hadn't trained for days and suddenly became very anxious. His drunken haze gave way to panic and he decided to redouble his efforts in the final hours before his meeting.

This increased training regime and self-imposed sobriety helped clear his mind and granted some mental clarity, but it could not help him escape the irrefutable truth. He had spectacularly failed in the task given to him. The way he saw it, he had but one choice. He was going to lie.

On the month anniversary of his second conversation with Doctor Shen, Josh again endured the long journey to his clinic. Arriving around seven o'clock, he found the Doctor as he had done the morning of his instruction, practicing Qi Gong in the adjacent clearing.

He stood still and waited for him to finish.

With his hands again coming to rest on his lower dan tien, he spoke.

"Have you completed your training as I requested?" Doctor Shen asked.

"Yes, Doctor Shen, I have." Josh replied.

The doctor slowly turned around, taking a brief look at Josh and shaking his head. In a slow, measured tone, Doctor Shen responded.

"You still have no idea of the questions you must seek to find the answers you need. I attempted to help you but you couldn't follow the simplest instructions. And then, in addition to this, you bring me lies. You have no shown no respect for me and no respect for yourself. I hope that you can find some peace in this life, Josh, as I can no longer help you."

chapter 8

After facing the disappointment of Doctor Shen's rejection, Josh recommitted himself to the perilous path of sex, drugs and alcohol that had contributed to his current predicament. Again feeling totally bewildered by his mental state and his surroundings, he could only bring himself to seek escape. However, Josh found that the problem with seeking solace in a bottle is that long after all the mind altering effects have left, the initial motivation for the bender remains. Repeatedly, his ill feelings were left amplified by the added discomfort from his body's recent toxic bath.

Josh knew that he had failed in his quest. There was no one else to see and the only one who had the answer he sought would never see him again. He realized that he should return home and try to reconstitute the broken shards of his life, but such thoughts distressed him so deeply that he was unable to leave. Thus, he dismissed all plans that arose in his mind and settled for any and all immediate external gratification available to him.

It was while walking this path that he found himself in Wong's bar, heavily inebriated after consuming half a bottle of Jack Daniels whisky. Wong's bar looked as if its interior hadn't been touched since its birth. The paint was discolored and peeling off the walls in places, with mold scaling the ceiling. The dim lights were not enough to hide the noticeable filth that pervaded the place. This was all of little concern to the clientele, who were there for cheap booze and some short relief from their day to day existence. The long bar was the only thing that seemed to have been maintained, its polished cedar wood surface incongruous with its derelict surroundings.

Josh had been sitting at the bar for a couple of hours when he noticed a pair of attractive women sitting at a table behind him. In his drunken stupor, he fell backwards off his chair and proceeded to lunge in their direction, with a failed attempt at saying "You're cute" in Chinese.

The pair giggled at his advances, obviously finding the western drunkard fascinating and surprisingly not displaying any signs of feeling threatened.

Josh smiled as he steadied himself on a nearby pole and proceeded to continue his amorous effort. Feeling increasingly confident from the alcohol and the seemingly positive results thus far, Josh walked over and placed his hand on the back of a chair at their table, fashioning a crooked smile on his face.

As he was about to sit down he suddenly felt a pull on the back of his head. Before he could react, his face was thrust forward into a bowl of nuts on the ladies table, scattering them into the air. Dazed, he rolled over and looked up to see two men standing over him, one bald wearing a white shirt, the other taller dressed in a t-shirt and jeans. The pair of women looked on, standing behind the men. Realizing their obvious relationship and unable to talk his way out of the situation, he thought it best to leave immediately.

Unfortunately, his two assailants had other plans. As Josh stood, one sent his left leg hurtling into Josh's stomach. Josh lurched forward as the other followed with an open hand strike to his face, propelling him backward into the bar. Heading towards unconsciousness, Josh's eyes were feeling increasingly heavy, shimmering light flickering throughout his vision. He managed to partially stand, resting his back on the bar and supporting himself with his arms. He raised one hand in a defensive posture over his face and readied himself for the next assault as the men again bore down on him.

As the bald attacker began to swing his fist, he was grabbed from behind by a third party. Turning around, the attacker was greeted with a series of kicks to his face, quickly rendering him unconscious. With his friend lying on the floor and the women screaming behind him, the taller man hesitated. The new fighter stood motionless, standing low with legs spread wide and hands held out in a defensive martial art pose.

Becoming increasingly nervous and with the women now crying, he turned in frustration, shouting at them to be quiet. He then suddenly lurched forward, propelling his fist at the new combatant. Easily avoiding the attempted strike with an efficient side step, the hooded figure unleashed a powerful sweeping kick, striking the attacker's leg and sending him falling to the ground. He stumbled to his feet only to receive a series of short, sharp strikes to his left shoulder, lower chest, upper abdomen and throat, with the final strike in the series incapacitating him.

Josh managed to hold onto consciousness long enough to witness the intervention of this good Samaritan. Appearing as if spliced directly from the reel of a Hong Kong action film, his final lingering thought before succumbing to the alcohol and beating was surprise that a middle aged woman had come to his rescue with such vigor.

He awoke in the bed back in his hotel room with a severe headache, a couple of cracked ribs and a swollen face. Putting down his hazy recollection of the previous night's events to a series of spirited hallucinations he was quickly brought back into the present when a woman's voice filled the room.

"There are so many potential problems with drinking excessively Josh, although I guess you don't need to be reminded of this now, do you?"

He sat up in his bed and turned toward the voice. He felt like he was caught in a vortex, the room spinning rapidly as waves of nausea moved through him. He let go and flopped back on his bed. The woman walked over to his bedside and sat down.

"The funny thing is, I know one often drinks to escape one's problems. This is something I have never understood, as it often seems to have the opposite effect."

"Some temporary memory loss of yourself and your life is worth the headache," Josh shot back in the most argumentative tone he could muster.

"Really now? I don't think you'll convince me of that when you are clearly not convinced yourself."

Josh rolled over in his bed to avoid facing her.

"Who are you and what do you want?" Josh sulked.

"I understood that you were on a journey of self-discovery. But it seems that I was clearly mistaken," she said.

"I was. Until this old man put unrealistic expectations on me and wouldn't tell me what I needed to know. Now I have no idea what I can do. I can't go back to my old life..."

"Why not?" she asked.

"I just can't. Nothing makes sense there. No one knows me anymore there. Hell, I don't even know myself anymore."

"So what were you trying to accomplish here?"

"I just want to find my friend. I thought that if I could find him and talk to him, apologize for what I have done and seek some guidance everything would be okay.

Now I have no way of finding him and therefore, no hope." Josh buried his head in his hands.

"Part of the trouble with expectations is that they are seldom met," she commented.

"I know. I should live in the present, I know. But how is that going to help me now. My present is awful. And that's beside the point, you didn't answer my question. Who are you and what do you want?"

"I think the present is exactly the point. The point of everything, all that is and all that will be. Eternity can only be accessed from the present moment. But to answer your other question, my name is Shupin."

"Why are you concerned with me?"

"Because I think my husband was too harsh."

"Your husband!"

"Yes. He has always accused me of being too soft and forgiving, and maybe I am. But I tend to agree with the great English poet Alexander Pope when he said 'To err is human, to forgive divine.' Fei Hung is a man cut from the cloth of the old school of Chinese masters, with discipline, respect and regimented practice at their core."

Now switching to self-pity, Josh said, "But he was right, he didn't ask much of me and I failed dismally. I procrastinated away my time and didn't do what was asked."

"I do agree with my husband's values, too. They are all important if one is going to actively pursue a spiritual life. Indeed, if one is going to have any life of significance such values should be held in high regard."

"Does he know you're here?"

"No, he does not. Fei Hung has certain expectations of people and the world that often aren't met, often leaving him riddled with disappointment. He has lived a life devoted to spiritual development and service to others from his youth and sees this world spinning more and more out of control due to the many excesses of our age. But rather than making him more lenient towards people affected by this, belief in his principles has been strengthened.

He holds that people have the right to choose in this life, with those choices leading to the karmatic consequences that follow. I don't see things so black and white."

"But isn't he right? We all do have choice and should be responsible for our actions."

"Of course we should, but I think most of us don't have the strength to choose as we could due to the information soup in which we swim."

"What do you mean?" Josh inquired.

"Take Fei Hung. Here is a man with high spiritual ideals formed over a lifetime of training. From a young age he was apprenticed to a master, with whom he studied and worked daily, training in Chinese medicine, Qi Gong, Taoism, Buddhism, Confucianism, calligraphy and Feng Shui. He had no real exposure to the outside world, no television; he didn't even really mix with children his own age! The only window into the greater world was through his English instruction, something his master foresaw as important in the coming new world. His precisely structured environment allowed his attention to be highly focused. This is how it has been throughout history and is the exact opposite to the conditions we have today."

"I know, we have many distractions."

"Well that's an immense understatement! We don't just have distractions, but we have people from all over the world telling us what to do, what to think, what to buy, what to wear, even how we should feel!"

"But surely we are still free to choose?"

"Yes, there is a choice made deep within each of us to do what we do. But the relentless external pressure applied on us all to choose to consume, indeed, to choose not to think for ourselves, is all pervasive! Only a strong, trained mind can hope to have any real choice in such an environment."

"Why do you think so differently to your husband?" Josh asked.

"I grew up in a small village in China, where again, I was relatively free of distraction. My parents were adamant that I studied hard so that's what I devoted my mind and my time to, for many hours a day. I was a good student and did well, and became fascinated with the study of English.

So, as I was due to finish high school, I applied for a scholarship to England and was accepted. Now you must understand that I had never lived in a large city, even in China, so I was unprepared for the contrast in lifestyle I was to experience in moving to London."

"So what happened?"

"I was taken aback by the sights and sounds as soon as I left the plane. I had never seen so much wealth!

The first time I went to a supermarket I was left dumbfounded by the amount of choice one had. I remember standing in front of the butter section for 30 minutes! It was then I had my first impression that an abundance of choice may not always be a good thing."

"How can you say that? You were just saying that we lack the real freedom to choose now, so how can having many choices be a bad thing?"

"Having choices for choice's sake is not real freedom. If there is no negligible difference between 10 products other than their names and the colors on their packaging, then it hampers your ability to choose, by not offering any real choice, just pseudo-alternatives."

Josh took her point, nodding slowly but quickly stopping when it seemed to bring back his feeling of vertigo.

"Anyway, I found it difficult to adjust to this new life, and found myself longing for the simple life I enjoyed in China. Most of my fellow students were friendly but their lives seemed to be run by one distraction after another, from the ubiquitous TV that seemed to be always flickering in the background, to the endless procession of gatherings centered around the consumption of drugs and sex."

"Hang on. I understand that that must have been a huge culture shock for you. But I had some of the best nights of my life at such 'gatherings'."

"I could see by some of the facial expressions I witnessed that my classmates would probably hold similar sentiments if they were here. I guess like everything, it's a question of balance. And from what I saw this was totally absent from most of their lives, going from one party to another. Their studies always relegated to the night before examinations, so information can be regurgitated to pass but then is soon forgotten.

Such distractions can prevent us from any kind of reflection on the current course of one's life and leaves you devoid of insight. There is plenty of time for a social life and study and work. Often I think people unconsciously avoid doing things that will bring about change in their lives. We live in the most quickly changing time in history and people cling to any constant they can find. Take you and your recent experience, you have no work, no real commitments except the couple of hours of Qi Gong prescribed to you by Fei Hung, and yet you still couldn't manage to do it. Why do you think that is?"

Josh felt uncomfortable with the attention focused back on his recent actions, his eyes quickly focusing away from Shupin.

"I have no idea. I started well. I practiced consistently for the first few days. But then one day I was a bit scared by some of the things my training brought up in me, so I went out for a drink and missed a session. Then, for some reason I didn't find time to do it another day, which I wasn't that concerned by as I had been so good. But those absences quickly multiplied, and before I knew it my month was almost up. It seems ridiculous looking back on it now, a pretty easy task to obtain the information that I wanted."

"Our collective propensity for self-sabotage is something that seems to have been cultivated especially in the modern era. Maybe it has something to do with the culture of instant gratification we find ourselves in. We are taught to believe that if something is of any value it should be able to be acquired quickly and easily. If any real effort is required, it is not worth the trouble. I see this in the pursuit of celebrity for celebrity's sake and the proliferation of reality TV. People are now so desperate for fame that they do not care how they arrive at their destination, as long as they are famous! The world seems to be upside down and turning in on itself."

"But surely everyone appreciates that any real success is the product of long periods of work."

"Do they? Do you?"

"I've worked hard to get where I am today."

"And yet we are sitting here at this moment of time where your path has been blocked due to your lack of effort. Many things have been accomplished by people who are working hard to avoid what they are destined to do"

She paused a moment, allowing the statement to percolate within Josh's mind.

He was struck by the fact that she seemed to have summed up his previous 10 years in a single sentence.

"We live in a time of instant gratification. You have a headache, so take a pill to fix it. You don't like your job, quit. You don't like your partner, get a divorce. You can't afford everything you want, get a loan. Forget the consequences; you can have anything you want now. This kind of thinking does not bode well for disciplines such as Qi Gong. Being a subtle art, signs of progress will only manifest over long periods of time. With no moment of arrival experienced, there is only a memory left of where you have been and how you felt in the past.

At its essence there is no goal, other than to rediscover your essential essence, something we all are taught to forget. With all the pressures that exist in our society it is no surprise that here in its birthplace, Qi Gong is treated as an esoteric outcast compared to more 'normal' pursuits, like tennis or badminton. It is seen by many of the youth of today as something that only old people do."

"So can you help me convince Fei Hung to tell me where Zach is?" Josh asked expectantly.

"I cannot convince my husband of anything that is contrary to his inner code. The thing that has failed you has been a sense of discipline; I can teach you something about that that may help."

"Please, anything that can help. I don't know what else to do."

"Surrender is good but expecting your problems to be solved by others is dangerous Josh. Something to be watched. I can help you but you will be doing all the work yourself. And I am sorry to say that this path is a lot harder than the one Fei Hung asked you to walk."

"I am ready."

"We will see. Meet me in the Red Dragon pavilion at five o'clock tomorrow morning."

"Okay, I'll be there."

With that, Shupin stood up and left the room, leaving Josh alone once again.

With a reinvigorated determination, Josh arose at 4 o'clock the next morning. He prepared himself and made his way to the pavilion.

The early morning air was cool against Josh's exposed skin as he walked quickly, aiming to be the first to arrive. His footsteps rang out over the sleeping streets. He was the only conscious human present, awake along with some cats rummaging through exposed piles of garbage.

As he approached the pavilion entrance he could see Shupin had already arrived. She was performing a series of martial art postures, fluidly moving from one to the next with deadly precision. His approach from behind caused her to end her form prematurely, drawing to a close by standing up straight and slowly guiding her hands down the front of her body, with the palms facing towards the ground. Her hands came to rest on the now familiar lower dan tien.

"Thank you for joining me Josh, are you ready to begin?"

"Yes. Thank you again for your help."

"I hope you will still carry that sentiment in a few hours," she said. "What do you know of the martial arts?"

"Not too much," Josh replied. "I know that knowledge of martial arts can be very effective in a physical confrontation, regardless of your size or the number of your opponents as you proved so succinctly yesterday."

"That is very true. When one is properly trained, one can use the Qi of your opponent against them. By subtly shifting your center of gravity and redirecting their force it can be enough to take them off balance and to the ground, giving them time to reconsider their course of action."

Josh nodded his head in recognition.

"Diligent practice of martial arts can also help cultivate virtues such as respect, focus and self-discipline. It is this last virtue that we are going to be working on as it is the one you seem to be having the most difficulty with."

Shupin went to her bag and produced a large white clock, with black, bold numbers carved around its edge. It had black hour and minute hands, with a prominent second hand in red. She came back over to Josh and propped it up on the table across from him.

"Now I am going to teach you one of the most fundamental stances of the martial arts. It is called Ma Bu or horse riding stance."

Shupin walked over to stand in front of Josh, between him and the clock.

"Josh, please stand up straight with your feet shoulder width apart."

Josh readied himself, following her instructions.

"Now, turn both your feet to point out..."

Josh turned his feet.

"...and then turn your heels out as well so that your feet are again parallel."

Following her instruction, Josh now stood with his feet about three feet apart.

"Now, drop your hips down, so you are standing in a seated position."

Josh dropped his hips, with his left knee letting out a loud crack in response to the added strain.

"Good. Now curl your hands into fists and place them on your hips, with the back of your hands facing down."

Josh again followed her instructions, feeling some initial strain seeping into his thighs.

"When you manage to hold this position for fifteen minutes, please ring the bell three times and I will return."

Josh thought about what her request entailed and was about to ask a question but she had already turned and walked away.

"Fifteen minutes is not long! How unfit does she think I am?" Josh wondered. "This will be no problem."

He remained in the position that Shupin had left him in as pain continued to increase throughout his legs. Lactic acid surged through his blood vessels creating an increasing burning sensation. He looked up at the clock. Only thirty seconds had passed since he had commenced.

"Maybe this would be harder than I thought..." Josh said to himself.

With sweat building and a tremor now evident through his body, Josh continued. He closed his eyes, trying to will the pain away. A voice arose in his head, "Stay in the present." Anger suddenly burst forth, with Josh saying out loud "Now why would I want to do that with the present being so painful!"

He let out a cry and fell to the ground. Looking up at the clock, he saw the result of his efforts. Three and a half minutes.

Josh sat in silence, reassessing his task while resting his legs. He realized that this was it, his final chance to find Zach. His final chance to find some resolution to this quest he had been compelled to take, whatever that might be. As his determination to find his old friend remained, his choice was already made. He briefly stretched his legs and sat back into the stance for a second attempt.

Josh's day continued in much the same way, with attempt after attempt after attempt. As the sun was beginning to set, he decided that he was done for the day, already realizing hours earlier that this was something that would take some time. He had managed a record of just over 5 painful minutes. He hobbled home along the path and collapsed in his bed, forgoing dinner for the peace of sleep.

The next morning he awoke to an incredibly stiff lower body. Muscles that he had never felt before cried out in pain with every movement he made as he slowly prepared himself for another day of staring at the clock. Despite this, a subtle shift had occurred. He knew that no amount of bodily discomfort was going to dissuade him from the task at hand. This acceptance did not eliminate the pain he was experiencing, but made it bearable.

Days quickly passed, with Josh settling into a familiar routine:

Wake up.

Morning training.

Lunch.

Afternoon training.

Home to bed.

His time steadily climbed as the days passed, with the pain in his legs easing as they gained strength. When he finally watched the clock pass fifteen minutes he couldn't quite believe it, but happily collapsed in a heap anyway. Looking up at the sky at the passing clouds he smiled with pride at his accomplishment. This changed when he realized that now he would have to demonstrate to Shupin.

"What if I don't make it in front of her? I barely made it then! Will that be it? Will it all be over?"

Finding this possibility unacceptable, Josh decided that he had to keep training. He needed to guarantee to himself that he could easily replicate his feat in her presence.

So he kept going. Pushing himself further, beyond fifteen minutes, he was able to reach the time with confidence after a couple more days. He awoke the next morning feeling fresh with only minor pain in his legs. He stretched beside his bed, stood up and smiled. This was the day.

He briskly walked down the path to his training ground, his companion clock under his arm. He arrived in good time, placed the clock in its normal position and walked to look up at the bell. He felt a sense of déjà vu staring at the bell's old, bronzed surface. Shrugging this off, he walked to its rope and pulled it three times. The three gongs unleashed sound that travelled throughout the surrounding trees, sending nearby flocks of birds into flight. Josh walked back to his training position, stood still and waited.

His wait proved to be quite short, with Shupin appearing minutes later.

"Excellent, Josh, congratulations! How do you feel?"

"Glad that it's over to be honest," Josh replied.

A touch of disappointment passed through Shupin's eyes. "Okay then. How did you feel as you grew stronger in your stance? What did you notice?"

"Well... obviously the pain decreased over time..."

"Obviously," Shupin agreed.

"... and this may sound strange, but as it got easier, my body seemed to feel lighter. Does that make any sense?"

Shupin smiled warmly. "Yes, Josh, that is excellent."

She continued, "Aside from cultivating discipline, this stance training is used to cultivate a strong connection with the earth. To 'grow your roots'. If you cultivate a strong root, it will help keep you grounded in all aspects of your life. And, in combat, you can become as solid as a mountain, with your opponent unable to shift you off balance."

Josh pondered what she had said. "That does make some sense, as at times I felt like I was actually sinking into the earth."

"Exactly. That was your Qi sinking, Josh. As you train, your Qi seeps out from your Lao Gung points..."

She held up her foot and placed her finger two thirds up from her heel in the center of her sole.

"From here, your Qi travels down into the ground, with Qi from the earth seeping up into your feet and up your legs, like sap rising in a tree. This transfer of energy is what creates this powerful connection with the earth and through your brief but diligent training, you have begun to cultivate this."

"Wow!" Josh said proudly.

"The more in touch with the Qi from the earth you become, the more the earth's energy will help support you in your stance. Thus, the easier that this will seem. As you continue to train, you will also notice that subtle shifts in your posture will produce a more effortless position.

As your bones increasingly shift into alignment it will be your skeletal frame that will support your weight, not the force of your muscles holding you there. Again, this will make your stance far stronger and easier to maintain."

She stood up and walked in front of Josh.

"Let me show you a small variation in your stance that can enable powerful Qi cultivation. This is a root stance of many forms of Qi Gong and Tai Chi."

She moved into horse stance, closed her eyes and let out a deep breath. Shupin then raised her arms out in front of her, with her elbows slightly bent. As if holding an invisible barrel in front of her, her arms were rounded, with her palms facing back towards her at the same level as her heart. Her fingertips from each hand hovered a couple of inches apart.

She opened her eyes. "This is called Embracing the Tree."

Josh dropped into horse stance and mimicked her position.

"That's good. Now really breathe into this stance, identify with your root and allow the Qi to surge up from the earth, through your legs, up your back and into your arms. Allow the earth to hold you."

Josh closed his eyes and visualized his Qi sinking into the earth. His stance dropped and he felt his presence sink.

"That's it. Now keep practicing that until you can hold it for forty-five minutes. Ring the bell three times and I will return."

Josh was concentrating on his stance so did not appreciate what Shupin was saying until she had already left. He opened his eyes to find himself alone again, only the memory of his new task still lingering.

"Forty-five minutes!" he thought, the very idea enough to send discomfort back throughout his entire body.

He stood up out of his stance and walked around. "Will she ever tell me what I need to hear? Is she even Fei Hung's wife?" These paranoid thoughts began to plague him. As his thoughts began to take him away from the task at hand, a small voice beckoned him.

"Come back to your breath... come back to your breath."

He left the mental chatter that had taken over his mind and focused on his breath.

In.

He felt the cool sensation of air pass through his nose.

Out.

He felt his breath pass over his top lip and down his body.

Another thought popped into his head, "How can I remove focus from my mind, when I am my mind? I think, therefore I am?"

The small voice returned, "Come back to your breath..."

In.

He could feel air pass down the back of his throat, filling his lungs.

Out.

His stomach and chest moved in and relaxed.

He continued this focused concentration for some time, with his eyes having long drifted closed. Feeling calm again he allowed his eyes to open and brought his attention to his surrounding area. Light from the sun was beaming through the tall tree in front of him, bringing the separate rays that managed to penetrate its leaves into focus. He could feel a gentle breeze on the back of his neck, lightly moving his hair and the leaves that surrounded him.

He felt at peace.

He again thought of the task before him. This simple shift of perception had transformed what he was to do from an insurmountable obstacle into something that he could easily accomplish, one step at a time. He reflected on Shupin's words and realized that rather than some arbitrary test, this was merely another exercise in his expanding repertoire, all dedicated towards his continued spiritual development. He smiled.

Josh settled into his stance in front of the large timepiece and raised his arms with a new resolve. On his first attempt, it was not long before he found his arms growing incredibly heavy, with his shoulders straining under their increasing weight. Rather than this frustrating him, he merely smiled and continued on, concentrating on his breath. He could feel the Qi rising up his legs and permeating his whole body. This sensation quickly brought his mind back to make comment on his experience:

Wow, I can really feel something.

What does this mean?

What is Qi?

I wonder what I will have for lunch today.

My shoulders really hurt.

So do my legs.

I have so much longer to go.

I can't do this!

These thoughts distracted him from his task and quickly intensified his experience of discomfort. Noticing his wandering mind, Josh brought his attention again to his breath and attempted to relax into his stance. With this focused attention, he was able to hold his position for some minutes more.

Josh again settled into a familiar routine with the new task he had before him. With the passing days he felt an increasing strength building in his legs and body and a greater connection to his surrounding environment. He felt his Qi drive deep into the ground, with Qi from the earth seeping up his legs, up his spine and circulating through his arms. He was beginning to appreciate the value of small shifts in his posture and the massive effect that they would have on his Qi flow. This always translated into a more effortless pose, further grounding him and bringing him closer to his goal.

This subtle training continued for some time until one day Josh opened his eyes from a particularly deep meditative experience and saw that he had held his stance for just over fifty minutes. He smiled.

Slowly coming out of his stance with a deep focused breath, Josh stretched lightly as his focus gradually settled on the large bell above him. A mix of emotions came over him, happiness, relief and fear all taking turns occupying his attention. The anticipation of the end of his quest stirred up familiar fears within him again.

"Will Zach be able to help me? How will I go back to a normal life?"

He knew that he had already gained immeasurable benefits from his journey thus far, but the sense of the unknown was still foreboding. He rang the bell three times and sat cross legged to await Shupin's return.

Some minutes passed with Shupin not arriving as she did before. Josh continued to sit, waiting patiently, resting in the present moment. After some minutes more, a young girl appeared in the distance, skipping towards him. Josh bowed his head in acknowledgement and used his minimal knowledge of Chinese to greet her.

"Ni Hao," he said.

"Ni Hao," she replied, unable to contain a broad grin. She was obviously fascinated by the presence of a Caucasian male, her serious facade failing her. She reached into her pocket and produced a folded piece of paper, which she placed in his large hands.

"Xie Xie," Josh said in thanks.

The girl giggled and turned away, running back towards the town.

Josh opened the note and read.

"Please come to the address below at seven o'clock this evening."

The remainder of the note contained Chinese characters, unintelligible to Josh.

He let out a sigh of relief. Some doubt had begun to rise within him during his wait, with the note quickly alleviating all traces. He saw that it was only two o'clock and decided to head back to his hotel to rest and prepare for the evening.

After having a short nap and shower, Josh headed outside and caught a cab to his destination. Following an hour's journey, the taxi stopped at a traditional moon gate as the driver gestured to Josh that they had arrived.

Josh took a deep breath, opened the door and stepped out onto the road, with the taxi quickly leaving. He was outside a freshly painted white outer wall with some tall bamboo stalks present to his left and right. He approached the circular wooden door and knocked.

He was greeted by the same young girl who gave him the note. She immediately giggled upon seeing him.

"Ni Hao," she said.

"Ni Hao," he replied. She motioned for him to come in. She ran in front, leading him into a well-lit dining room where Shupin was waiting.

"Welcome to my home, Josh, and congratulations! How do you feel?"

"I feel very well. Thank you, Shupin."

Josh let out a deep exhalation. He had finally finished.

"Shupin, I must ask, why did you help me?"

"Josh, the most important thing we can do in this life is be of service to others. I was merely following this basic axiom of life."

"If that is the case though, how can what I am doing now be seen as the best way to serve others? I am walking a selfish path to try and find some peace in myself by finding my friend?

She looked down and smiled, lightly shaking her head.

"Therein lies the paradox – from one perspective the path of service is a selfish act as you gain a sense of inner worth and satisfaction that is incomparable to anything else! From this good feeling you become compelled to serve more and so on and so on..."

"I see," Josh replied.

"Also, adequate time must be spent on self-development so one can best serve others. If one devotes all their time and energy to service early in their life, one may hope to serve and influence a thousand people. If one were to devote sufficient time to developing traits such as self-mastery over mind and body, only then using this wisdom to serve, you may impact millions, with your influence lasting generations."

Josh sat in silence, reflecting on Shupin's words.

As Josh began to speak, Fei Hung appeared around the corner.

"I see that you have sought to redeem yourself young man." Fei Hung said.

Josh bowed his head. "Only because of your wife, Doctor Shen. I again apologize for not completing your task."

Fei Hung waived his hand in the air. "That is the past, Josh. It is a waste of your Qi to dwell on it. Nothing will come of such a preoccupation."

Josh nodded his head, with his eyes facing down, hesitant to look directly at the doctor.

"I can see now that you have had some small success with your training. Don't become complacent with small victories. There is no end to the path of spirit once begun. It is only in consistent, daily practice that you will find any solace from the ills of the world."

"Yes, Doctor Shen," Josh agreed.

Shupin nodded her head in agreement and reached across the table to pour tea for the group.

"May I now ask about Zach?"

Doctor Shen sighed and closed his eyes for a moment.

"Your search for Zach has helped bring you onto a path of self-development which has been good. However, as I said before, do not become obsessed with outcomes and don't be focused on expectations of future events. This can only lead to a life of misery and disappointment. You will soon meet Zach and you must let go of attachments to find true value in his teachings."

Most of Doctor Shen's speech was lost on Josh with only the words, "You will soon meet Zach," still ringing in his ears. He could barely contain a smile signaling his excitement.

"Zach trained diligently here for some time and was an excellent student. His main failing was an obsession with the outcome of his path, obsessing over the fulfillment of an end spiritual goal. He wanted to 'arrive' at the end destination, to finish. This fixation prevented him seeing that he had already arrived. Indeed, that we all have arrived as we have never really left..."

Excitement now turning to mild frustration, Josh could make no sense of Doctor Shen's cryptic speech. His mind was solely focused on the information that he was promised, the knowledge that had driven him all over the world. He had to ask.

"So, exactly where is Zach?"

"He is in Japan, living in Tokyo. He went to train with one of my master's there."

Josh sat back in his chair in relief, the knowledge that he had long sought now obtained. Now only time separated him from his old friend.

chapter 9

Josh stepped off the plane into Narita airport once again, overwhelmed with emotions. He was elated to think that his search was finally over and he was to soon see his lost friend again. But he also felt a sense of apprehension as to what the meeting would actually bring. Given the circumstances in which they last met, he wasn't even sure if Zach would be keen to speak to him, let alone help him with his current existential crisis.

Trying to avoid dwelling on such questions, Josh did his best to bring his attention to his breath and the unfolding world of Japan around him. He had always enjoyed his travels to Japan and expected that this trip would arouse similar feelings.

He made his way to the baggage collection area, picked up his belongings and was soon on the Narita express train bound for Tokyo station. Scenes of vibrant green fields filled the windows of the train soon after exiting the airport, always unexpected so close to the mega metropolis that is Tokyo. These would soon morph into a condensed urban vista, a complex array of roads, buildings and technology filled with people engrossed in their daily lives.

After an hour the train arrived at Tokyo station. Josh left the train and made his way to a nearby taxi stand. After a short taxi ride, he was soon in his hotel room, preparing himself for his meeting. After a quick shower and change of clothes he sat down on the bed and grabbed the hotel phone, placing it on his lap and holding the receiver. He let out a deep sigh as he looked down, reaching across for his diary and flicking through the pages until he came to the long sought information. Another deep breath entered and then slowly escaped through his lips and he typed in the numbers before him.

The phone rang once.

Josh held his breath.

It rang a second time.

He continued to hold his breath in anticipation.

The phone began to ring a third time and was picked up.

Josh's mind began to race, only to be greeted with an unintelligible string of Japanese words from a voice recording. His excitement changing quickly to exasperation, Josh hung up the phone and released a long sigh. Fortunately, he also had Zach's address. So, armed with an old photo of Zach, he set off.

Arriving at a well-worn concrete building, Josh managed to find an old couple who recognized the photo. He struggled to communicate with them due to their low level of English and his non-existent Japanese. They finally led him to another apartment where they believed someone knew him. This was to start a succession of meetings animated by vigorous body language and a semi-coherent mix of Japanese and English, gradually drawing Josh closer to his final destination.

His series of enquiries finally led him to an Izakaya in the red light district of Kabukicho in Shinjuku. Josh moved past the ubiquitous red lantern marking the entrance and slid open the traditional wooden door. Taruichi was a traditional Izakaya in every sense of the word; deep red wood lined the walls, with small tatami floored rooms off to the sides filled with groups of drinkers. The bar carried an abundance of alcohol, with numerous kinds of sake and shōchū complemented by a wide range of beers and spirits from around the world.

Josh scanned the bar, looking for a Caucasian face. He didn't have to look long but those he found were not his friend. Thoughts were bubbling up within his mind questioning why would Zach be here, but as he had little else to lead him he continued his scan. He spotted what appeared to be a western man slumped over the end of the bar, perched on a stool. Josh approached him from behind and tapped him on the shoulder.

"Excuse me," Josh said, clearing his throat.

The man slowly turned around and met his gaze. It was Zach.

"Joshua Black! How the hell are you!" Zach said, leaping out of his chair with an overzealous hug for his former friend.

Clearly inebriated, Josh was taken aback by this greeting, patting Zach on the back in their embrace and managing to say, "It's good to see you, too."

Zach's forlorn appearance was completely incongruous with the image Josh had built up in his mind. He was expecting some kind of spiritual warrior, someone who would help him vanquish the demons in his soul and send him off into a life filled with light. Instead, here was a man with blood shot eyes, scotch tainted breath and a slumped posture, barely managing to keep himself seated on his stool.

"So what brings you to Tokyo?" Zach began. "Hang on... where are my manners! Sumimasen! A drink for my lost friend here! What'll you have?"

"A water would be fine..."

"Water! I don't think so! After all this time..." he turned to the barman. "Another two scotches, and make them doubles!"

The barman quickly poured the drinks. "Come Josh, let's have a seat."

Zach led him over to a corner table with two vacant seats.

"So..." Josh started.

Zach beamed back a drunken smile, "So yourself! Look at you! It's great to see you. So how's the life of the rich and successful treating you? What brings you to Tokyo?"

"Ummm...", Josh started, shifting uncomfortably in his chair, "actually, you brought me here."

Josh explained the series of events that led him to the Izakaya where they both sat, starting with the plane crash. As his story unfolded, Zach's facial expression gradually morphed from that of a smiling drunkard to a man possessed by depression. After he had finished, Zach sat, eyes down, shaking his head.

"You shouldn't have done this," Zach said.

Given Zach's current state, the same thought had briefly crossed Josh's mind. Sitting there staring at his friend, he could not yet process the ramifications of their unfolding meeting.

"Why not?" Josh asked.

"You've come to me for answers? I don't have any answers, at least none that anyone wants to hear."

"Why happened to you Zach? How could you not have found some truth on your search? In my brief time searching for you I have experienced moments of insight that I'm still amazed by..."

"Well, in the end Josh, I found out I was wrong. You know way back when we pursued our separate paths, deep down I thought I knew. I had this confidence, this arrogance fuelled by some dark part within myself, that I knew best, that I was chosen to have this knowledge. I looked at everyone around me, including you... especially you... and thought that you all had such meaningless lives. I was the spiritual one pursuing a life of meaning..."

Starting to laugh, Zach continued, "... but I was wrong, Josh, and you were right. Damn the world and everyone in it, concentrate on making yourself happy, that's all there is. So you were right, congratulations!"

He raised his glass gesturing towards Josh and poured his drink down his throat.

"But that can't be true, Zach. I wasn't happy. And that is what has brought me on this trip, on this search for you."

"Before your little near death experience you were happy enough, I'm sure. Money, women, power. You need to go back there Josh cause that's all you can get. Just hope to rise to the top of the sewer that has become this world."

Josh couldn't believe what he was hearing.

"You don't honestly believe what you are saying? Do you?"

"Why not?" Zach replied. "You cannot honestly look at the world and tell me that the rich and powerful don't have the best deal of all. Basically all the world's resources are exploited by a handful of people, with the rest of the population from the 'developed' world sedated into submission to continue powering the whole machine by running on their little hamster wheels. And they're the lucky ones... at least they have food, TV and alcohol to numb them from the repetition of their mindless jobs. The rest of the world struggle to get enough to eat, or are living with bullets flying past their heads on a daily basis, wondering if the next air raid siren will signal the collapse of their house from above."

Josh struggled to find something to say, as Zach continued.

"Your life before you hit this little psychological bump in the road was pretty good, wasn't it?

Lots of respect, enough money to buy anything you really desired, women at your beck and call.

How can you sit here and tell me that you didn't have it all? I should have been seeking you out, to get answers on how to live a good life from you!"

"But my life lacked any real meaning Zach. All the possessions and false praise and feigned respect really amounted to nothing at the end of the day. I was actually beginning to feel happy that I experienced my plane crash as the things I have discovered since then did seem to provide some sense of purpose, that I could do something with my life for the greater good. I just can't believe that after walking the same path and meeting the same people as I have you have fallen into this pit of despair."

"I am not in a pit of despair Josh," Zach replied. "I once thought like you but have since had my eyes open to the misery of the world. I can feel the masses of humanity crying out for some peace, so forgive me if I would choose an existence consumed by the pursuit of material desires over the many other miseries that can befall a human life."

Josh was shaking his head. "You cannot possibly believe this. Aren't so many of those miseries caused by the materialistic pursuits of the few?"

Zach stared back at Josh and clasped his hands in front of him. "You're right Josh. I am full of shit. But given that you had come all this way looking for some answers, I figured I had to make some attempt at giving you your previous life back."

"Yeah, well... sorry, Zach. You weren't very convincing."

"What can I say?" he replied, shrugging his shoulders.

"So, what is the answer then?"

"Haven't you now realized that I don't have any answers for you. I wasn't lying when I said that the world is slowly slipping into hell and we're the ones driving it there. So much misery and suffering surrounds us that I can barely stand to get up in the morning."

Zach stared ahead into nothingness.

Feigning a smile, he raised his glass and said, "So, that's why I drink!" throwing back the last of his bourbon.

"Are you serious?" Josh asked.

"Why not? It's the only real legally available opiate for my soul. In this hypocritical world of ours it has become the drug of choice for governments all over the world. So, it's easy to get and you don't encounter any opposition in constantly consuming it if you are relatively quiet and keep to yourself. Personally I feel that some more illicit substances would have a less damaging effect on society than the scourge that alcohol can leave. But the nefarious world that you must associate with to get access to them and the potential for imprisonment tends to leave a bad taste in my mouth."

"So you are saying heroin use is better than having a drink?" Josh asked.

"No, I didn't mention anything specifically, did I Josh? Obviously, heroin addiction when out of control can lead to all kinds of social problems, like burglary and violent crime when one has exhausted their resources and is driven by their addiction to score. All I am saying is that the violence and anger aroused in many people after a drinking session constantly causes destructive behavior in societies all over the world, whereas many drugs cause passivity like heroin, or marijuana, or even states of universal love, like ecstasy. At least these users will be only harming themselves – not dragging others into their den of iniquity such as those perpetrating alcohol fuelled street violence."

"So you want to legalize all drugs then?" Josh asked in disbelief.

"That is not what I am saying at all, Josh. I am merely pointing out one of the many forms of hypocrisy that exist in our world today. And these hypocritical beliefs usually only exist because they have existed over history, usually formed at a time and place when we didn't know any better. But because of the sheep that we are, we all unconsciously follow the legacy of our forbearers, trudging along and wondering how we can stop making a mess of everything. It's often very easy, Josh… just stop doing it! Listen, let me put this to you…"

Zach moved forward in his chair and leaned over to Josh. His alcohol soaked breath now engulfed Josh's nose.

"Say I had a product for sale that I had devised that I knew was going to make me billions. It would be highly addictive, so I would have a very loyal customer base. It would also generate a lot in taxes for governments around the world, but it had the slight inconvenience of killing people through long term use. Do you think I would get approval to sell this product?"

"I know where you're going with this," Josh replied, "but to answer your question, no, of course you wouldn't."

"No shit. But yet the tobacco companies throughout the world operate with relative impunity. They have been found to have lied about their knowledge of the harmful and addictive effects of smoking for years. Indeed they used their knowledge of addiction to enhance the addictive qualities of their product to further condemn their users to a life of ill health and disease. And yet they still operate, with the world jumping through all sorts of hoops to lessen the use of their product. We ban cigarette advertising. We raise taxes on their products making it more expensive so people will struggle to afford it. We ban smoking in restaurants, bars, and public places."

"But all that is good, all these measures have helped decrease the amount of smoking in the world," Josh stated.

"Yeah, maybe, but hey, here's a solution: BAN THEIR SALE AND SHUT DOWN THE COMPANIES THAT PRODUCE SUCH A LETHAL PRODUCT FOR PUBLIC CONSUMPTION!"

"But it's not that easy..." Josh began.

"Ah, the classic retort. It's not that easy... hmmmm... really, why not?"

"Ummm, well there are must be many reasons. Like people's jobs..."

"Another common defense of all kinds of wrongdoing in our world today. Of course people need jobs. But, it is a very large leap between the necessity of jobs for people and the value of any particular one job. A JOB in and of itself does not have ANY intrinsic value. You see on the news when a company is shut down and they report that 55 people have lost their jobs. This is always presented in a somber tone, like the sky has fallen in. Now I am not understating the difficulty imposed on some in the search for employment, but we forget humans are adaptive creatures, we can be re-trained or re-skilled in fields where workers are required. We all fear change, but in the end, change is all that exists. Are you telling me that some tobacco employee is not better off, both in themselves and for society, if they have been re-trained as a teacher or a nurse? Actually giving back to society, rather than being part of a state sanctioned murder squad?"

"Okay, but what about people's free choice? Shouldn't people be able to choose what they do?"

"So, then why can't we choose to consume other illicit drugs? Or why does a person's freedom to choose justify a company producing deadly products? Here's an easy solution. If you want to smoke, how about you learn how to grow a tobacco plant? It will be a lot better for you without all the noxious additives that the companies add, and maybe it will inspire you to learn about horticulture, hardly a bad thing. But with humans the way we are today, most people's venture into gardening would be short lived or they wouldn't even try in the first place. So, either way, they would give up their nasty habit!"

"Maybe, but it's not going to change," Josh replied.

"Untrue, everything does and will continue to change. Just not in ways we may wish it would."

"I guess that's true. So what is the answer then? Isn't the search for spiritual truth the reason why we are here? To live a religious life?"

"Live a religious life? Ha! One of the most hypocritical aspects of our collective psyche," Zach laughed.

"Come on, surely a religious life is a necessary good in this world. There must have been many moments of good on your path for you to continue along it for so long?"

"Don't confuse the terms religious and spiritual, Josh. Often the most religious people are the least spiritual, while others who have never even contemplated following a religion deeply spiritual. One of the many problems with the world today is that religion has hijacked the realm of mainstream spirituality. It has done so for centuries. We seem to forget that all the mainstream religions have pasts littered with examples where their followers have committed atrocities against humanity in the name of their version of 'God'. If someone was to try and rebrand the ideology of Nazism by disavowing themselves of the massacre of the Jewish race, but upholding its basic tenets, the general populous would look upon them as abhorrent. But nothing is said about, for example, the billion or so people who follow Catholicism, which was responsible for countless massacres throughout Europe during the crusades. Islam is decried in western media as a violent religion, but the religions with which it shares its roots, Christianity and Judaism, both share equally violent pasts."

"Hang on, but the majority of followers only really concentrate on those positive attributes of their faith, like, love thy neighbor as yourself, and 'turn the other cheek'..."

"True, but Judaism, Christianity and Islam all recognize the Old Testament of the Bible as a Holy Book, inspired by the word of God. Have you actually ever read the thing? My God!

One of the most violent and depressing texts my eyes have had the misfortune to read. Littered with talk of slavery, and God sending plagues on the masses. And you will always hear intolerant Christians quoting scripture from it to highlight the 'evil' of homosexuality. If you turn to the next page, you will find a passage about how it is okay to stone your slave if they try to leave your care! Are we all insane!? How do you think society would react if they were to quote such passages in their defense of slavery or some sadistic form of corporal punishment?"

"I imagine not too well," Josh replied.

"Of course not. Some of the most spiritual people have never attended a formal religious ceremony. Whereas some of the most religious are the most intolerant, bigoted people one could meet, very far from any noble spiritual ideal such as being more 'Christ-like'. God is the only one who is supposed to stand in judgment of humanity, and yet some religious people constantly judge others according to their moral code, mentally or verbally condemning them. Their smug superiority makes me sick!" Zach ranted.

"It sounds like you are speaking from experience!"

"Josh, I'm sure you have experienced such things as well but your former egocentric existence probably didn't even notice! I constantly see supposed religious leaders who have climbed the hierarchy of their establishment who don't exhibit even one iota of anything that could resemble spirit. These are the men responsible for covering up child sexual abuse in their churches, responsible for the continuous ostracizing and condemnation of the gay and lesbian population, responsible for the marginalization of women throughout history. And these men are close to God? A God who sits in judgment and approves of such bigoted intolerance and simultaneously condemns a kind, compassionate person simply because they have never attended a mainstream religious establishment is a God not worthy of worship!"

"Do you think people honestly believe that?" Josh asked.

"Of course they do, it's one of the ways people can justify sitting in judgment of others. 'They don't share our belief but that is okay because God will punish them for it and we'll be rewarded for eternity in heaven.'"

"I don't think it's that simple…"

"Of course it isn't, but that doesn't matter. Many people think this way, this is how they perceive the world, and let me tell you Josh, perception is everything."

"Well I don't perceive the world like that," Josh replied, with a slight air of superiority.

"Of course you don't, Josh. You have your perceptions filtered by the government and the media, so what you believe is different but equally limited. You read about some war in a far off country and think you are informed, you think you have an idea about this world that you live in, but let me tell you, you have no idea."

"How can you say that? You haven't spoken to me for over ten years, you have no idea what I know or believe."

"Really? I bet until you started this whole journey you were quite absorbed with your own life, the acquisition of money and the growth of your business. News of the world and those around you was provided through sound bites you would catch on TV between your dinner and dessert."

"You underestimate me," Josh replied half-heartedly, not believing his pitiful rebuttal.

"Maybe I do, but I doubt it. Our whole world is built up on people's perceptions. Take any crisis in the financial system throughout history up until this point. There may be external factors that start the chain of events but the most important point is that people lose confidence in the system, they perceive there is a problem, so people sell their shares. This causes a drop, so more people lose confidence, so more sell and so on. When you live in a token economy such as ours, where the only real value in any of our money is perceived value, it can operate in no other way. Governments take advantage of this, shaping what we perceive to be true, to disseminate their propaganda."

"Now, hang on. We don't come from a police state. Sure, politicians are often dishonest liars but our governments don't actively engage in spreading propaganda."

"Are you serious? From what you are saying it doesn't even feel like we live in the same world. We are all stuck in an Orwellian nightmare by our own collective implicit agreement and we can't even see it.

History is rewritten before our eyes to favor those in power, truths become lies and lies become truth, and all the while the world's poor and desperate suffer. The affluent minority are kept complicit as long as they are fed the latest junk food TV through their sixty inch flat screen. Take the 2003 invasion of Iraq by the 'Coalition of the Willing'.

There were many countries around the world at the time in control by tyrannical regimes, some worse than that of Saddam Hussein.

And yet, Iraq was singled out in the wake of the September 11 attacks as a regime whose continued existence threatened the safety of the world. Never mind that the intelligence to support the main supposition behind the invasion, the existence of weapons of mass destruction, was deeply flawed, and by all accounts, heavily influenced by the Bush Government to justify their invasion."

"You aren't suggesting that dictators like Saddam Hussein should be allowed to acquire WMD's are you?"

"No, but I'm making the point that it is equally unacceptable for any country to possess such weapons. The nuclear non-proliferation treaty had two functions. One was to prevent the spread of nuclear weapons to countries that didn't already have them, but the second related function was to preserve the status quo. This has failed by all accounts though, as Pakistan and India have both acquired nuclear weapons, with little consequences from the international community. Israel has a well-known cache of undeclared nuclear weapons and has done so from before the treaty was signed. And now the US, with its missile defense shield, looks to shift the balance of power away from the MAD doctrine..."

"MAD doctrine?"

"Mutually Assured Destruction. Quite a fitting acronym I must say. It can now be argued if the US can defend against a barrage of nuclear missiles and then fire its own retaliatory strike that the balance of power has significantly shifted. I personally think that this is highly unlikely. It is one thing to be able to shoot down one stray missile from the sky, but it is certainly another to shoot down ten, or fifty, or even one hundred missiles at a time. This is beside the point though. If there is a perception that the balance of power has shifted, then that is enough. So, another arms race may be started. It is just madness. Anything but global disarmament is absolutely unacceptable."

"Isn't that a little unrealistic?"

"Probably. But definitely not unreasonable. We live in this intimately interconnected globe where a few citizens from a few countries have the power to destroy us all. How dare anyone presume the right to that power? This power has been used once with devastating consequences to the people who experienced it firsthand. And now those bombs dropped on Japan are like toys compared to what is available now. It all makes me so sick!"

Zach buried his head in his hands and started rocking back and forth, mumbling to himself.

"Zach... Are you okay?" Josh asked, touching his shoulder.

"No Josh, I am not okay! How can anyone be okay? Are you not listening to what I am saying? The world is fucked up. FUCKED UP! And no one seems to give a shit. Do you have any idea the amount of people that are experiencing pain right now? I mean, really visceral pain, really suffering?"

"Uhhh, no, but I am sure that there must be a significant number..."

"Significant? Ha!"

Zach's cheeks began to turn bright red, with the color quickly spreading to the rest of his face.

"Millions, Josh, millions of people are all right now writhing around in pain. And that's just physical pain. Now add emotional pain and there are so many millions more!"

Zach's whole body started to spasm. His breathing became labored, with his exhalations becoming short, sharp, rapid bursts. He started to extend his arm as his hand contorted before him. The whites of his eyes filled their sockets as his eyeballs rolled back in his head.

Josh looked on in helpless disbelief. He tried to communicate with Zach but he was unresponsive. He quickly looked around the rest of the bar for someone, anyone, to help him. No one had even noticed the localized commotion occurring at their table. Just as Josh was standing up to shout for help, Zach's condition seemed to improve. His eyes closed and his arm relaxed to rest by his side. His breathing began to calm and soon all his previous symptoms seemed to have abated.

"Zach," Josh said. "Zach!" Josh grabbed his shoulder.

"Please..." Zach slowly enunciated in reply. "Please don't touch me."

His hands moved to rest in his lap, right hand on left with his palms facing up. He held this position for a matter of minutes, with long, rhythmic breathing.

Josh's mind was racing. "What the hell is going on?" he thought. Any quest for answers or help from this lost soul was obviously futile.

He just wanted to leave, but he knew leaving would place him in a position more removed from any peace than he had yet known. Zach opened his eyes.

"I need another drink, and so do you!" Zach said. "Sumimasen!" he shouted motioning toward a waiter.

He secured another round of drinks that were quickly brought back to the table.

"What just happened?" Josh asked.

Zach let out a big sigh. "That, my friend, is why you should abandon this whole quest you have put yourself on, and try to resurrect your former life."

"What? That happened to you from meditating?" Josh asked. "It seemed like meditating helped calm you down again to come back to normal."

Zach laughed. "What you just witnessed was very far from normal."

He took a large gulp of his scotch.

"In a different world, Josh, the path that I was on may have brought everything I sought. But the world is so sick, Josh, that it appears all I have managed to accomplish is infest myself with its illness."

"But Zach…" Josh started.

He raised his hand as he finished his drink. "That's enough. I don't want to talk about it!"

Zach swilled the remaining scotch around in his mouth, swallowing it with a large gulp.

"Josh, if you really want to do something meaningful with your life, go join a protest group, raise awareness of all the suffering and atrocities that our governments, our fellow humans, commit to each other and our planet!"

"Do you think that will help?"

"To be honest, no. But it may help you, because at least you would feel like you were doing something. Because if you continue down this road, you are going to discover all kinds of things about this world that you would be happier not knowing…"

"But I do already know that the world has its problems.

I know we have environmental challenges and human rights abuses to face."

"Challenges? My God, what you know would only scratch the surface. There is death and destruction going on at an alarming rate of humans, animals and the environment all the time."

"If that is so, why are these atrocities not openly reported? I can't believe what you are saying as it would take a huge conspiracy to perpetrate such a feat…. and you are not talking about one incident… you're suggesting that these things are ongoing, consistently occurring! How could we not know?"

Zach lets out a depressed laugh and shakes his head with a sad smile.

"That's just it! There is no conspiracy; these things are not reported out of the free choices of the media en masse! Sure, often things slip through the cracks of the media net in some place or another, but in general the mass media usually publish the propaganda line of the government in question. Dissident intellectuals like Noam Chomsky have published on this for years and do attract a small following amongst similar radical thinkers. But as for the public at large, these ideas are not present, and when they are raised, those that do are painted as unpatriotic or as communists! Communist: My personal favorite insult. Have you even heard of Noam Chomsky?" Zach asked.

"I vaguely remember something from first year psychology… I thought he had something to do with language learning?"

"Yes, in the 1950's he made a major contribution to the field of linguistics, turning the pervasive model of the time on its head with his proposal of innate language acquisition centers. This was in contrast to the prevailing 'blank slate' model of behaviorism from B.F Skinner. Basically he held that we are born with innate knowledge of the basic grammatical rules common to all existing languages on earth and it is from these building blocks that we're able to learn the languages that we do."

"Yeah, that's right. So how does he fit into what you're saying?"

"Chomsky has been a political dissident his entire adult life, writing on subjects such as anarchism, power and its abuse, global inequality and the media. He is most famous in his political writings for a book he wrote with Edward Herman called Manufacturing Consent."

"Sorry, haven't heard of it," Josh said.

"Why does that not surprise me?

Anyway, in it they talk about a 'Propaganda Model', an analytical framework which explains how the US media disseminates information based on the implicit wishes of those that own and control the media. This is accomplished not by overt censorship or government control, but by the hiring of 'right thinking' journalists and a system where reporters come to internalize the philosophies and values of their employers and their government so as to reflect the wishes of the powerful."

"Now hang on, it's not called a 'Free Press' for nothing. The media can report on whatever they like, an individual journalist can follow a story without being pressured against it. There are laws, constitutional protections..."

"Yes, that may be the case. And at times things are reported outside of the wishes of the powerful elite. It is not a ubiquitous system of control. But any of these stories of dissent usually remain at the margins, gaining no real traction and thus not penetrating the consciousness of the public at large. I'll give you a recent example of this. Take the 2003 Iraq war. In October of 2006, The Lancet published a peer reviewed epidemiological study on the number of additional Iraqi deaths due to the war during a period spanning just over two years. You want to know what figure they came up with? Six hundred thousand people! At the time, the US military had an estimate of deaths of around thirty thousand, to an absolute maximum of fifty thousand people."

"But how can that be possible? How have I never heard of it?"

"Obviously the study's results are controversial. But after being published in such an eminent scientific journal, with the methodologies used backed by epidemiologists from all over the world, you would expect the conclusions to be taken more seriously by the world's media! President Bush and General Casey were predictably dismissive of the results, but this dismissal seemed to be accepted as fact by everyone! The study dropped off the international media's radar within days!

We are talking about a discrepancy of hundreds of thousands of dead Iraqi's. And, as such facts are inconvenient for the invading forces, any investigation into these allegations doesn't seem to merit a mention in the newspaper. It's all there on Wikipedia, look it up!"

Zach shook his head as Josh sat listening in silence.

"The thing that really gets me is that in other conflicts, figures produced by this particular methodology are used without question. Like in the Congo, almost 4 million people were reported to have died in the conflict, with these numbers accepted by the US congress, the UK parliament and the European Union. It seems when 'enemies' are doing the killing, such horrific death counts are acceptable for print."

"I am speechless," Josh said. "I just don't get it. How can this go on? Journalists in democratically elected countries are free! If they pushed, they would be free to report on such things. Wouldn't it be good for the particular media, help them sell more newspapers or get more viewers?"

"People are not free to choose anything!" Zach exclaimed. "Every supposed choice we make is couched in a range of unexamined beliefs and assumptions about the world that, in essence, make the choice for us!"

"So you are saying that we don't choose to believe what we believe?"

"In almost all cases, no. Humans are creatures of habit, and our beliefs and assumptions are no exception to this rule. Hell, how can we choose to believe something other than we do, when we don't even recognize the beliefs that drive us in the first place!"

"I don't get it, how can we not know what we believe?"

"Our mental map of the world is complex, formed from childhood from a range of different stimuli. The most important influences are those that have some power over us, like parents, teachers or friends. This power can be of course exercised for good or ill. On top of that, we have companies directly targeting children to sell their products, attempting to insert a belief of the worth or value of their product into an unsuspecting mind. So, we come to like and dislike what we do through a collection of external stimuli, usually unchallenged by us. So in time there will usually cease to be a reason why we believe what we do, other than the fact that we have always done so!"

"We may be readily controlled as a kid, but if you're educated to have an inquiring mind, you're not as easily manipulated."

"You are speaking of yourself? What education are you referring to? It is true that if one is deeply contemplative of their beliefs, you can sift through the sludge and come up with some logical reason as to why you believe what you do. If properly executed, this process will usually result in one changing many of one's fundamental beliefs when their shaky premises are exposed. But sadly, this is far from the case for much of the populous, trudging through their existence seldom making anything like a free decision. People are driven by a mishmash of instinct and their ill-conceived assumptions of the world. Socrates once said, 'the unexamined life is not worth living'. By this definition the world is filled with worthless lives."

"Thanks for another depressing thought.

I assume that this is with the exception of the powerful, of course? So they're pulling all the strings then, truly in control?"

"Yes and no. The heads of business and government do direct the lives of the masses for their own ends, but this does not make them truly free. They too have their own set of unexamined beliefs and assumptions albeit different to the slave army they command. Often born into a life of privilege they may see their rule as divinely ordained, but they still accept their lives as they have been programmed, further perpetrating the social systems that came before them. Probably less likely to question anything as they are told by everyone that they 'have it all,' so why would they?"

Zach surveyed the people around him and then looked down at his watch. His eyes fixed on an attractive woman standing chatting with a group of her friends. She caught his gaze and quickly looked down, shifting her feet and producing an involuntary smile.

"Sorry, Josh. That's all the advice I have for you. I said that you should go back to your old life, but I can see that isn't possible. You can't unlearn these discoveries that you've been forced to make. Try to help some people, focus on your breath in times of depression, and just know that there's nothing that you can really do about this huge mess we find ourselves in. Look mate, I've got to go and use my Friday night. I think I might have a chance over there. I would say come and join me, but judging by your face you'd just be a downer for the group. All the best, Josh."

Zach slapped Josh on the back and made his way over to the female group he had been eyeing.

"ME be a downer? What just happened?" Josh thought, his mind struggling to comprehend what just happened.

chapter 10

Josh was devastated. He could not escape the incontrovertible truth: Zach had followed this path to completion and it had left him in a drunken mess. The diametrically opposed experiences that he had had were impossible to reconcile. He had felt a real sense of achievement, accomplishment, of purpose to his life that he had not felt before. However any positive feelings had been erased by his meeting with Zach. His presentation of humanity as a sick, corrupt institution unwilling to seek redemption, couldn't be true, could it? His arguments seemed unassailable. There was obviously good in the world, but humanity had been hijacked by the manipulation of our most basic impulses in an endless cycle of consumption that was destroying us. These thoughts whirled around his head as the final boarding call for his long haul flight home to Australia came over the loud speaker.

Josh stood up and surveyed his surroundings for a final time. Everywhere he looked he saw people utterly consumed with their lives. All embarking on international travel for one reason or another, all unconcerned with the impending doom that our species seemed to face. He longed for a time before this sudden detour in his life where he could be one of them again, where concern for the choice of his next drink far outweighed hopeless thoughts of planetary destruction and spiritual salvation.

He walked over to the boarding gate entrance and gave the attractive flight attendant his boarding pass.

"Thank you, sir. Enjoy your flight," she said finishing her statement with a small bow of her head. All Josh could muster in return was a grunt with a slight head nod. He had to get out of his head but he knew that was the only place where there was no escape. He hurried to his business class seat and sat down near the window. The only respite he could see was the world of sleep. He put his head back and was thankful for an instant as darkness found him.

He awoke to a jolt of sudden turbulence and the seatbelt light flashing overhead.

The nightmare of his previous flight home from Japan vividly returned to him with fear gripping his body.

"I don't believe we're going to crash again. Just some normal turbulence this time," said the man sitting beside him.

"Crash again?" Josh thought. He turned to face his seated neighbor, his jaw dropping as his eyes met his. He recognized him. He was the last person he saw on his doomed flight, the serene sage that manifested compassion at will.

"We were never formally introduced, Josh. My name is Tsuyoshi Yoshida."

Josh recoiled at the mention of his name. "How do you know me? What's going on?"

"Relax Josh, I'm not here to harm you," Tsuyoshi said. "I'm only here to help. I see that you finally found Zach. I hope you weren't too disappointed."

"Disappointed? More like stunned! My whole trip has been a waste of time. If that's how I'm going to end up I should have stayed home and wallowed in my shallow existence."

"We all walk a different path, Josh, and have different lessons to learn along it."

Josh shuffled uncomfortably in his seat, pushing against his arm rests, but unable to break eye contact with Tsuyoshi.

"How do you know me, and how do you know Zach? Have you been following me?" Josh demanded.

"In a manner of speaking, yes. I'm only here to help, Josh. I first heard about you from your friend, Zach, a couple of years ago. As soon as he mentioned you, I could feel the karmic residue between you both and knew at once you were to meet again. Indeed, that we would meet. Fei Hung let me know that you would be paying us a visit a few days ago, and I thought you may have some questions after meeting Zach... so, here we are." Tsuyoshi replied.

"Questions? You could say that!" Josh replied sarcastically. "For starters, why were you on that plane? Did you know it was going to crash?"

"I knew that there may be some trouble and I was only there to help. People benefit immeasurably from spiritual guidance and support in times of crisis like we experienced, even if it's only through another's supportive presence.

At first, when the scale of the disaster became apparent, I thought that it may be my time to leave this world, but after seeing you I knew that I had another student that needed some support."

"Are you insane? How could you know that? And if you did, how could you step onto the plane?"

"In your limited period of spiritual training I think you have been privy to knowledge that cannot be arrived at through the traditional senses. As one explores the world of spirit and the inner eye expands, your capacity to absorb information from other sources greatly increases."

"That still doesn't answer my question," Josh said.

"No, it doesn't." Tsuyoshi replied. Closing his eyes, he rested his palms in his lap and sat forward in his seat.

Josh looked at him with incredulity.

"So now you aren't going to talk to me, is that it?" said Josh, becoming increasingly frustrated.

"No, but I believe you have more pertinent questions to ask," he replied.

"Like about Zach?" Josh inquired.

"Yes..." Tsuyoshi said.

"What happened to him?"

Tsuyoshi opened his eyes and again turned to face Josh, leaving his hands resting in his lap.

"Zach is experiencing the unpleasant symptoms of 'Kundalini syndrome'. Do you know what Kundalini energy is?"

"Yes, I met a Kundalini yoga instructor during my trip."

"Excellent. Well, in Zach's hurry to experience enlightenment and unleash the ball of latent Kundalini energy at the base of his spine, he had what you might call, a misfire..."

"A misfire? What are you talking about?"

"Through force of will alone he managed to stir his Kundalini energy into action, but he hadn't done sufficient preparatory work so the awakening didn't go as expected for him. These higher level spiritual practices can actually be quite dangerous due to the nature and amount of raw prana one is working with. In the case of Kundalini, a misdirected manifestation can be experienced by the body as paralysis, psychosis, or even premature death!"

The plane again shuddered with turbulence, the approaching flight attendant grabbing a nearby seat to steady herself before resuming her meal service.

"He didn't appear to be crazy. Just obsessed with the doom and gloom of the world," Josh commented.

"That is because Zach experienced different symptoms of Kundalini Syndrome." Tsuyoshi answered. "Symptoms that I had never seen before but were his karma to bear. A universal consequence of an awakening, common throughout most mystical religious traditions is a visceral connection with all that there is. An experience of completeness. A knowledge that we are all essentially the same thing. We are all one."

Josh nodded his head in understanding.

"Zach has experienced a variation of this, but with an overt focus on all the pain and suffering being experienced on our planet today. We can all understand intellectually the trouble the earth and its inhabitants are in, but Zach has constant experiential knowledge of this fact. He feels the suffering of the world and can't turn this feeling off."

"My God, that sounds awful! Why don't you help him?"

"I tried to help him. He was my spiritual apprentice for two years before this happened. I never had a better student in many ways. He was highly motivated and dedicated to his training. Behind this though, was this unrelenting drive to succeed, to find answers, to 'solve' this life. I think this was rooted in the death of his sister. He was driven to make some sense of it, to reconcile his knowledge of the greater world with the horrible fact that his sister was taken so prematurely, for no apparent reason. He managed to mask this inner mania quite well most of the time, but I could see it at work behind the scenes, pushing him, forcing him to train harder, faster and driving him to accomplish his goal. I tried to teach him one of the many paradoxes of spiritual awakening; that one must train hard and diligently, but one cannot force the process. Enlightenment is not a state of doing, Enlightenment is a state of being!

Spiritual training merely provides the appropriate ground for any awakening to occur spontaneously. Trying to push too hard cultivates the potential for disaster, as Zach discovered for himself."

"So why aren't you helping him now?"

"I will be always here to help Zach, when he is ready to ask for it again. When Zach is ready, I know that he will be able to work through his current predicament. Coming back to the basics of his training, practicing being in stillness, encouraging balance, grounding his energy back into the earth... these are all things that Zach will eventually come back to, to bring himself back into alignment."

"He really needs to do something, judging by our conversation."

"What did he say?"

"He went on and on about the 'conspiracies' of the world, how there are no answers because we are all locked in the same prison, all controlled by the world we have created."

"Ah, I see. Well, unfortunately, Josh, I believe that what he told you is most likely true."

"What! But you said..." Josh began but was interrupted.

"I said that he had a pathogenic manifestation of Kundalini. I did not say he was crazy. Given his extraordinary perception, he has a greater capacity to feel the stark injustices of the world."

"So you agree that there's no hope? What the hell do I do now? I thought my life was ruined before, but this whole trip has made everything worse!" Josh said, lowering his eyes and shaking his head.

"I never said there was no hope. Zach is blinded by his negative focus," Tsuyoshi replied.

He leaned over and patted Josh's leg.

"There is considerable hope, Josh, and people like you are the key to it all!"

Josh balked at the suggestion and the implicit responsibility contained within his statement.

"But how can I be the key to anything?" Josh asked.

The flight attendant arrived at their seats with their meals.

"The only two vegetarians in business class! That's quite the coincidence, wouldn't you say?" she remarked.

"I would agree with that," Josh answered dryly.

Tsuyoshi allowed a small smile to appear on his face.

Producing their tray tables from their arm rests, they received their warm meals. Both thanking the flight attendant, she moved on to the next passenger. Delicious aromas of Japanese cuisine wafted upwards as they both removed their thermal packaging. Their plates contained a variety of Japanese dishes including Miso soup, tempura, harumaki, and a selection of shojin ryori, the traditional vegetarian cuisine of Japanese Zen monks. Josh began to salivate as the food fed his eyes and nose first, in anticipation of the taste of the varied dishes. He picked up the chopsticks at the side of his plate and started eating immediately, thankful for the brief break in his conversation.

Swallowing his first mouthful of rice, Tsuyoshi continued. "There is currently a clear bipolarization occurring in society..."

"You mean the growing gap between rich and poor?" asked Josh.

"No... actually, I was talking about the growth of a particular perception, a worldview. As the world we have collectively created becomes increasingly complex, fundamentalism is raising its head and becoming dominant on the world stage..."

"Like Islamic fundamentalism?"

"Yes, that is one breed. From a spiritual point of view, there are two distinct sides - religious fundamentalism, and let's call the other side, anti-religious fundamentalism. Religious fundamentalism is often discussed, especially in the context of Islam. This is, of course, closely followed by Christian fundamentalism, particularly that which is practiced by evangelicals in the United States. You can define this as a dogmatic adherence to a specific set of religious beliefs, with this fixated view preventing the follower from seeing the world in any other way. This has been the cause of so much conflict throughout history, continuing to this very day."

"Okay. So with anti-religious fundamentalism, you are talking about scientists?"

"No, but there are scientists that follow this world view, with Richard Dawkins being an example. He's probably the most famous atheist of our time."

"So, atheists then?" Josh asked, as he picked up his bowl of soup to drink from.

"No, I'm talking again about people that hold so steadfastly to their particular belief system that they are unable to see anything outside it."

"I know what you mean. I actually discussed this with a former scientist. People can get so invested in their set of beliefs, their paradigm, that they can't see anything else."

"Exactly. Within the realm of modern science, there lie sets of assumptions taken as sacrosanct, with anything falling outside this taken as patently untrue. For example, the current obsession with 'double blind placebo controlled trials' in the medical world. If one can't satisfy this 'gold standard' of scientific inquiry, then any kind of investigation performed is suspect. Never mind that there may be many bodies of knowledge that do not lend themselves to this particular method of proof. Or that results are sometimes manipulated, findings only reported when they fit with the research organizations wishes. For example, how can one apply this 'gold standard' to a new surgical procedure? Do you want to volunteer to be in the 'sham' surgery group? Of course, the biggest exponents of this method are the pharmaceutical industry where it is easily applied, and can be used to continue justify the massive amounts of money produced there."

Tsuyoshi took a mouthful of seaweed, rice and vegetables and chewed them thoroughly, as Josh digested both his food and the words that had been spoken.

Swallowing, Tsuyoshi continued. "Also take any knowledge gained through introspection? This is seen as subjectively flawed by many scientists, but throughout the ages many ancient seers used this method to learn numerous universal truths. But the real reason that two such diametrically opposed camps have evolved is historical. Most major religions continue to demonstrate their unwillingness to change unless under considerable external pressure. They deify a few ancient documents, often riddled with factual inaccuracies and archaic beliefs that seem insane to many people. Thus, the rational camp finds it easy to sit back and ridicule or pity the poor fools who are taken in by such obvious charlatans. It's religion's historical quest to maintain its power that has inadvertently created the view held by so many scientists that the spiritual world is a myth. Hundreds of years ago in the face of an exponential rise of scientific influence, religion attempted to maintain its authority over the divine by cordoning off the physical world as the domain of science.

This was only conceded so the spiritual realm was left as the exclusive providence of religion. In doing so, religion sowed the seeds to its own downfall. When scientists demonstrated that their knowledge of the physical world could explain everything far better than having to resort to a belief in an unprovable supernatural being, religion lost its tenuous claims to authority in the eyes of many. It is only now through a reversion to a more fundamentalist ideology that many mainstream religions are finding power once again, to the detriment of all."

Josh scraped the last of his bowls for any remaining remnants of food, pondering Tsuyoshi's words.

"But I don't get it. How is religion finding power in fundamentalism?" Josh questioned.

"It seems the more complex the world becomes, the more people turn towards fundamentalism in an effort to understand the world through some simplistic belief system. Everything makes a lot more sense if you are given a fixed, finite set of beliefs about the world and rules that one must follow. Coupled with the promise of eternal life in paradise, one has good reason to want such things to be true. Similar things can be said of an anti-religious fundamentalist. The current set of scientific principles is held to be the keys to absolute truth. Thus, their belief system may evolve and change within these carefully defined parameters but it is still couched in overarching assumptions of materialism, immediately dismissive of anything deemed 'spiritual'. Personally I find this as hard to believe as the views of a religious fundamentalist, given my experiences and the extraordinary world painted by modern Quantum physics."

"But the two 'sides' you are talking about are not all that there is. I'm sure plenty of people have less rigid beliefs, on both sides," Josh commented.

"Indeed. As is so often the case, the middle way is the most logical. Not holding to the dogma of either side, the middle way is free to marvel at the discoveries provided by modern science and can appreciate the deep truths advanced by the various spiritual traditions of the world. It is supremely arrogant to write off all spiritual practice and belief cultivated throughout the history of man as some kind of collective delusion designed to deal with our mortality. And yet it is infantile to blindly hold to strict beliefs prescribed by ancient texts that were written in a different time for people in a very different set of circumstances."

Finishing his food, Tsuyoshi quietly placed his chopsticks down to one side.

"The dogmas of religion and materialism will one day fall to the tenets of reason and spiritual experience," Tsuyoshi stated.

"How can that be possible? People hold so strongly to their religious or non-religious beliefs. They become part of their identity. People define themselves as Muslim, Christian, or Atheist... I can't believe that this could change like you're suggesting." Josh argued.

"Individual spiritual experience not couched in any particular religious tradition can open one's eyes to the beauty and wonder of the world. The unity of all life and the magnificence of all creation.

A move from the current adversarial nature of our society to one where co-operation and the nurturing of our essence as inherently creative spiritual beings would revolutionize our planet. We make artificial borders, we carry remnants of past conflicts, past grievances all commenced by individuals that have long passed. All these things are taught and passed down from generation to generation, but nothing tangible exists! The beauty of relatively new, truly multicultural nations like the United States, Australia and Canada is that one can witness the evaporation of past conflict in all strata's of society, but especially so in children. I think one of the most beautiful sights is that of a kindergarten class in a multicultural city, walking as a group, gathered in pairs, holding hands. They are a kaleidoscope of races, of nations, of histories, all walking hand in hand, oblivious to any historical hate or distrust. They are all simply children. And the sooner we all realize we are all just people, living together on this beautiful rock called earth, the sooner we can all truly enjoy this experience, this gift called life in all its wonder."

"Some people have wanted this since time began, but this hasn't brought it any closer to happening," Josh replied. "You have those on one side who are so bitter, carrying hate and perpetrating violence, and then those on the other side who are totally indifferent to everything, content to ride on the coat tails of civil society, taking all they can and not giving anything back. And then there is everyone in the middle who have to deal with the repercussions of both sides. It's not fair!"

"The dissatisfaction of people who condemn those that waste their lives doing little and survive on handouts is predicated on the idea that most people do not like what they do, but yet tolerate it, because 'they have to'. Thus, those that choose to do nothing and act as the proverbial parasite on society are inherently bad, especially as their lives may secretly be seen as desirable by those who are perpetually dissatisfied with their own.

A life that they cannot have, or else they relinquish their martyrdom complex. The martyr works, they do the right thing, even though they hate what they do. In a world where people are actually fulfilled in their lives, such individuals who disengage from society would be viewed with empathy. The disengaged would be actively coaxed into service so that they may have as equally fulfilling a life as the rest of society, rather than whittling away their limited time on our planet."

"So you think we have the time and resources to support people leading such lives?" Josh asked skeptically.

"The world does not have to work in the way it does. It is the relentless drive of consumerism that feeds the growth of the working week, driving us forward to make more money so we can consume more products. The hidden fact of our world is that if we weren't so driven by this mindless urge to consume, we could all work much less. All the technology that we have created could be used for its intended purpose – freeing us from menial tasks to give us more time. The average working week could be at least cut in half, so we would have a large part of our lives back to spend as we will. This could mean more time with our families and friends, more time to explore life's great questions and follow our real passions. Some may argue that this would mean a devolution of our society. I would have to disagree. It would merely be a change of emphasis from a greed, consumption driven society, to one driven by our inner potentials. One would have the time and energy outside work to pursue our passions and ideas, enabling society to evolve on a wholly different and more fulfilling tangent. Some people have realized this, downshifting their lives and forgoing many of the trinkets we now deem as necessary to live a simpler life, with less unsatisfying work and more time..."

Their flight attendant quietly approached, taking their empty trays away.

"But all this innovation, all of the technology that would make that possible is produced by the system of market capitalism. It doesn't work without constant growth," Josh objected.

"That is not true. The innovation and evolution of technology throughout our history is produced by our brothers and sisters of earth, our fellow human beings. Capitalism may have been used as a device to organize and motivate humanity but it is our essential creative drive that can be credited with our advancement. As a system, capitalism has been effective in producing somewhat efficient and internally cooperative systems that run our world today.

We must not forget its many shortcomings though, producing massive inequalities between people and nations, prompting mass exploitation of both people and the environment. The fundamental premise of the entire free market system is hopelessly flawed, assuming that the consumer is entirely free to choose and has perfect information about the market in which they live."

"So are you saying we should become socialists? Or communists?" Josh questioned.

Tsuyoshi laughed and shook his head. "Not at all. But is it sacrilegious to propose that an alternative model may be found that would work better for humanity? Many are so paranoid about questioning the economic status quo that they quickly revert to a 1950's McCarthy style inquisition. Things are far from perfect in the world as we all know it, and current orthodoxy should always be questioned in a search for something better."

"I can appreciate that. I guess you just have to look at the financial meltdown of 2008 to see that there are problems."

"Exactly. We have lost sight of what society could be striving to accomplish and have become restricted to what we have been taught is possible. We collectively learn our society's perceived limitations, so they forever remain self-fulfilling. Just as we learnt women were inferior to men, black's inferior to whites, natives inferior to colonists... we learn that it is impossible to have universal healthcare, we learn that excellence in education for all is too expensive. We learn that whomever is blessed with the money has the rights to all and those that aren't make do with the little they have and the 'generosity' of the country they find themselves born in. It is amazing how it is acceptable to put a price on healthcare and on education. Those that are able to pay get the best, those that aren't, something else, if anything at all, all down to the whims of the 'market'."

"But you have to put a dollar amount on things so people will value them," Josh said.

"Really? What is more valuable to you, Josh... a relationship that you pay for or one cultivated over time through values of friendship and mutual respect?"

"That's not the same thing!" Josh protested.

"I'm merely illustrating that value is not intrinsically linked to the almighty dollar. Our education system fundamentally shapes the world in which we live.

It saddens me greatly when I see a price tag affixed to it, brandished as a political football. The catalogue of human knowledge and experience is not something that can be bought and sold, it is the birthright of every individual on this planet."

"But people have a right to make a living from the things that they invent, things that they discover!" Josh retorted.

"Yes they do, but we must frame their discoveries within the context of history. We don't recreate calculus every time an engineer wants to estimate the structural integrity of his design under different circumstances. Calculus is a gift to the whole world from the minds of Newton and Leibniz. Everything we learn and discover now is based on how fortunate we have been to access a quality education, to access the teachings of those that have gone before us."

"I had never thought of it like that," Josh admitted.

"Imagine how far you would have got in your life not being able to read, let alone not having mathematical skills. And then there are the innumerable subtleties that shape you through practicing problem solving and critical analysis throughout your schooling. So much of a fulfilled life is owed to the constant nourishment and expansion of the human intellect and, yet, intellectuals and educators are often derided in societies in which they are present!"

"So I guess I have been lucky then..." Josh said.

"In so many ways, Josh. You have had this access to education that so many crave, and you have lived in a healthy environment with advanced modern healthcare available to you, should you fall sick. We now have the technology and resources to open the knowledge book of human experience to all corners of the world, not just an advantaged few. We are inquisitive by nature... this natural curiosity could be satisfied for our entire lives through global universal education. We also have the knowledge and resources to take care of the medical needs of our planet. We all know that millions die daily from easily preventable diseases, to our collective shame. These are not questions of money! This is merely a question of our collective will."

"But aren't you being too idealistic? There would have to be massive international agreement on an unprecedented scale to accomplish anything like what you're talking about."

"The idea of such international co-operation being beyond humanity is patently untrue. We demonstrate vast international consensus on a daily basis. Take air travel. We have literally thousands upon thousands of international flights going on, twenty-four hours a day. From the initial act of booking a flight, this requires co-operation between travel agents, airlines and airports from all over the world. Think about the massive coordinated effort of airplanes physically entering the territory of other countries, all sharing one or two runways for a particular airport. Then the act of passengers embarking and disembarking their particular flights, with their luggage in tow. All this requires co-ordination internationally on a massive scale, but when travelling we don't give it a second thought because it's usually so seamless. Look at us both sitting here on this flight now. It is just a normal part of life."

"It isn't always so seamless." said Josh, thinking of his doomed excursion months prior.

"True, but even then, if one is subject to an accident like we were, rescue teams will be coordinated no matter where such an incident might take place. International agencies coordinate together to provide relief as soon as possible for those affected. If you put your mind to it, I'm sure you can think of countless examples of international cooperation that have had impact on your life."

"I appreciate what you are saying. I agree that we can cooperate when it's seen to be in our collective self-interest, but when it isn't, cooperation seems impossible. The global free market capitalist system here makes gains that were previously unable to be made diplomatically or politically... hence demonstrating its validity, as it speaks directly to people's individual self-interest."

"Does one's individual survival not speak most directly to one's self interest? Or global peace?" Tsuyoshi asked.

"Yes, it does..." Josh agreed "...but it's obviously not that easy."

"I agree. But if we are to avoid a state of global misery, the likes of which has not yet been experienced by humanity, we are running out of time. Talk of global catastrophes and religious predictions of Armageddon have been with us for millennia. But never before have we faced such a dire prognosis on so many fronts."

"You sound like Zach," Josh observed.

"Well, I'm afraid there are reasons to be pessimistic. And the single greatest cause of our current global dilemmas can be traced to the disproportionate rates of social and technological evolution around the globe."

"I'm not sure what you mean?" Josh asked.

"We are obviously evolving technologically, at an increasingly rapid pace. We have also made significant social progress around the world on a number of issues. In both fronts we are moving forward, but at vastly different rates. This is something that threatens us greatly. If our awesome power to destroy ourselves, by accident or through intent, is not tempered by an evolution to a comparative level in social organization, global misery will envelop us, continuing for centuries to come."

"But we are progressing socially..." Josh began.

"Of course we are. There is no doubt that we are progressing socially. Think of where we have come from: slavery, the oppression of women, different rights for different classes of people. In many quarters of the world there has been a substantial shift over the last century to a more egalitarian society. Many overly focused on the woes of the world and the declining nature of our society seem to forget this."

"But things are getting worse, crime is on the increase and people have less respect for each other now than they did in years past." Josh interjected.

"True... due to the loosening of social constraints, the decline in the community structure and the proliferation of heavily addictive drugs, there has been some increases in criminal activity. But one must temper this with the increase in reporting criminal acts that has increased exponentially. For example, sexual abuse in the past was something that was covered up and not discussed, therefore, was seen to not exist."

"I take your point. That is something that we know not to be true now, given all the cases of abuses by priests that have come out."

"Yes, and of many others. People are now in an environment where it is okay to talk about what happened to them in the past and bring justice to those who perpetrated such heinous acts. So my point is we have come a long way, in many ways. Who could have imagined that we have come so far as to have a person of mixed race elected president of the United States!"

"So how is this a threat to us then? Now you make it sound like we are doing great as a species?"

"I am merely highlighting the significance of the social change that has taken place. I am not saying that we don't have a long way to go yet. And therein lies the problem. Great gains have been made socially, and yet we continue to repeat the same barbaric behavior that has defined us as a species for centuries – stark inequality between people and murderous war constantly being waged throughout the globe. Virtually all nations, whether rich or poor, developed or developing, seem to see killing others as something that is a justifiable right!"

"But sometimes nations do need to go to war for the greater good," Josh replied

"I wouldn't put it like that. In those times where there truly is no alternative, war isn't something to be celebrated. The taking of another's life for whatever reason one can produce is always an evil act, sometimes it just happens to be the lesser of two evils. The simple truth is as humans we are still killing each other as we have done since the beginnings of so called 'civilized society'. We may come up with all sorts of justifications as to why this is the case, but this does not change the fact that we are still killing! And with our rise in technological prowess we have become increasingly sophisticated in doing so. This is another example of the inherent creativity of humanity, although it is being funneled into production of extraordinary examples of death and destruction. Billions and billions of dollars are spent on this every year by all nations of the world. The fact that this is seen as acceptable shows we still have a long way to go."

"But isn't that just human nature?"

"Perhaps. But I don't believe so. I think it is human nature to live in peaceful co-existence with one another. The vast majority of the world wants this. Many lucky countries have this. But until we can have this on a global level, humanity will forever battle the demons that remain from our past."

"But we seem to dwell on the misery of humanity. You say that many countries live in peace, but in those countries many still seem to dwell on any death and destruction that they can."

"That is very true. From an evolutionary standpoint one could understand how it would be advantageous to be compelled to share news of death and destruction of others for one's own survival. This proclivity of humanity has become engorged by constant feeding from the global mass media.

We are saturated daily with the various woes of the world, both real and perceived. We revel in the misfortunes of others, particularly the Gods of celebrity that we both worship and cut down in the same breath. This daily dose of hyped up global misery has a huge effect on all of us throughout our lives, affecting our thought patterns and our potentials. Imagine if some of this massive media machine was directed to provide us with uplifting and inspirational stories that surround us daily. But such stories remain in the shadows due to the erroneous belief that it is only misery that makes money in this world."

"That must be the case. If one thought that the news was a proportional representation of all that is going on around us we would be living in a perpetual war zone, all dying of disease, obesity or famine, with crazed celebrities causing public spectacles wherever we looked!" Josh exclaimed.

Tsuyoshi laughed. "Exactly! I think this disproportionate representation is clearly evident with the religions of today. All the great spiritual traditions have wise masters, living and working within local communities throughout the world. These priests and monks, rabbis and nuns, often share similar qualities of compassion and tolerance, leaving a lasting impact in all those exposed to their heartfelt teachings. Through their humble nature, these beautiful souls are seldom recognized by the world at large, content to carry on their works in the shadows, their lives firmly devoted to the service to others. You have movements within Catholicism like Liberation Theology; fighting the causes of poverty, social injustice and human rights abuses. However, these movements are too often condemned by the church hierarchy and are seldom reported on in the western media. What we do hear about constantly are those that spew hatred and intolerance and preach an abomination of their prophet's teachings. These maniacal clerics and their vile words only gain greater power through their constant exposure via the mass media. This is especially the case in Islam, with all the good done by countless Imams' throughout the world undercut daily by the crazed rants of a select few."

"So what's the answer? How is any of this going to change?"

"As I said before, people like you are the key to an unprecedented era of peace and prosperity for the human race."

"I still don't see what you are talking about."

"Only by a global shift in perception, a shift away from our outdated beliefs and our unnecessary prejudices, can we come to realize the magnificence of the potential of humanity.

Through a global spiritual revolution, with individual seekers experiencing their own truths in the world and living in peaceful co-existence with our planet do we have hope."

"Do you think that this is possible?"

"This is already occurring. For example, we have the rise of inter-faith ministries across the world, showcasing the rich variety and beauty across a range of religious traditions. They embrace the multitude of paths available to us, trading traditional exclusivity for an inclusive approach. We have various non-government organizations throughout the globe working tirelessly for the collective good. NGO's like Amnesty International, fighting for the rights of everyone, particularly those that can't fight for themselves; Médecins Sans Frontières working all over the world in some of the most inhospitable and war ravaged regions to bring healthcare to the needy; Friends of the Earth, the world's largest grassroots environmental NGO working to restore and preserve our natural environment, in the hope that one day human beings and nature can live together in true harmony. There are literally hundreds of organizations like these and millions of individuals, working all over the world for the greater good, all trying to do their part to build a better future for us and our descendants. It's just a question of whether their collective movements can gather enough momentum in time."

"How do you think that this could happen?" Josh asked.

"Through collective spiritual experience. The key spiritual truth that must be experienced by a critical mass of people is the fact that we are all connected, we are all one. Our intellectual understanding of this is clearly not enough. Intellectually, it sits as an idea in our consciousness, along with a multitude of others, competing for attention, if it's thought about at all. When this knowledge is felt, experienced permeating our very being through spiritual practice, it informs every action we take, every word we utter. We can't help acting in accord with the greater good of our planet. I believe you had some experience with this?"

"Yeah, I guess I have. I had glimpses of what you're speaking about, but all only very fleeting."

"Sit back, Josh, and close your eyes." Tsuyoshi asked.

"Wait, what for? The last time I was asked to do that, it did not end pleasantly," Josh said hesitantly.

"Don't worry, Josh, just put your chair back, close your eyes and relax for a moment," Tsuyoshi reassured him.

Josh pressed the side control on his seat and eased himself back into a reclined position. Closing his eyes, a nervous blackness overcame him as he waited for what was to come. The familiarity of the loud drone from the plane's engines soothed his mind as he resisted the urge to fall sleep again.

Tsuyoshi began to speak in a slow, measured rhythm.

"Take your attention to your breath. Let your attention dissolve into your dan tien."

Josh moved his focus to the area below his belly button.

"Breathe in."

Josh took in a long, slow inhalation through his nose.

"Breathe out."

Josh released his breath through his mouth.

"Bring your attention to your clothes. Feel the weight of your shirt press against your skin."

Josh could feel the subtle touch of cotton on the hairs of his forearms.

"See the journey it has made to find itself draped over your frame. From cotton fields in the United States, India, China, Africa and Brazil, all requiring sustenance from the soils of the earth and rain from the heavens, cotton is grown and harvested. Spun into cloth and again transported to and from all corners of the globe, one is perceptually ignorant of one garment being made from material picked by hand by children in Northern India or harvested by machine from a farm in South Eastern Australia. See the many paths woven through time and space, the many hands that handle, the many minds that determine, the fate of a simple piece of clothing you casually select from your wardrobe."

Josh's mind bounced around the globe following the multitude of possible paths taken by his humble shirt.

"Breathe in deeply."

His attention returning, he felt a dry, cool rush of air through his nose.

"Exhale deeply."

Josh released a torrent of air with an audible sigh.

"Feel deep within your body. Focus on your stomach. Feel your last meal being consumed, the hydrochloric acid of your stomach tearing the food apart. Unrecognizable from what you placed in your mouth, your digestive juices break your food to pieces, into smaller chemical parts, nutrients all ready to be taken by your blood, pumped throughout your body. Our globalized world delivers this food to your hand, to your body, millions of people throughout your life you will never share a meal with, a conversation, or even see their face, all providing your sustenance, all a link in the global chain that is your food supply. The fruits of their labor are now melding with your body, becoming an integral part of your being. Proteins from the soya beans made into the tofu from your meal will be integrated into the muscle fibers throughout your body, repairing you, strengthening your physical form. Your rice is broken down into carbohydrates, then into glycogen, serving as fuel for your body. The various vitamins and minerals from your vegetables all play their part in a complex chemical dance, seamlessly choreographed all without the attention of your consciousness."

Josh's abdomen made a brief perceptible growl, aware of the smooth muscle fibers of his stomach rhythmically relaxing and contracting, churning its contents.

"Let your attention drop, deeper again as you inhale. Relax your body."

Josh sank further into his seat.

"The water you drink has been raised by the sun from seas on the other side of the world, taken by winds travelling at the edges of the globe, finally delivered to catchment areas near your home and stored in dams fashioned by the hands of man. This constant cycle of renewal, from the seas to the land, to the rivers and back to the sea, has been going on since the beginnings of life on this planet. These ancient processes supported the possibility of humanity for millions of years before our eventual arrival."

Josh's mind travelled from land to sea, from river to dam, following the flows of water with Tsuyoshi's words.

"Similarly with the air we breathe, our forests that have provided us shelter and food, all exhale the diatomic oxygen that is vital for all our lives. We move through our environment as if moving through empty space, where in reality we are bathed in gasses that comprise our air. The delicate balance of nitrogen, oxygen and carbon dioxide that is our air, is made by life, shared by all life, sustaining all life. Feel the air around you as it sits on your skin, moves in and out of your lungs, providing you oxygen, providing you with life."

Josh continued to breathe deeply. The pressurized air from the cabin had a slight chill to it, cooling his throat and causing the small hairs on the back of his hands to stand up.

"All of our actions affect all of these systems, both the systems we have created, and the systems that created us, because we are a part of the system, part of the interconnected web that is earth, that is life. From the smallest single cell bacteria, to the largest mammals on the planet, all life has its place, all life has its purpose within this intricate tapestry. When one species dies, or one forgets its natural balance, all will be affected, effects spreading like the ripples from a stone dropped in a pond. This is most blatantly evidenced by the rise of homo sapiens, and how destructive our disproportionate domination of the globe has been. We may choose to act in harmony with our world, or in discord; with our home reflecting our choices back to us like a mirror."

Tsuyoshi paused for a moment, allowing Josh time to feel the pull of the infinite threads of the surrounding web.

"Nothing else exists but our perception of our world. Right now you are sitting peacefully, our perceptions, our mental experience of the world is fed locally, but connected to everyone, to everything on our planet like never before.

Every time we come within the sensory range of another, we become a part of their perceptual landscape, impacting lives in both major and minor ways. A smile witnessed by a stranger leaves behind its imprint, as does a voice raised in anger. Like ripples in a pond, the inconsequential to us can reach out and affect lives well beyond our comprehension. These causal chains are enhanced by our media. Now through technology, one individual can spread hate or love directly to every corner of our planet in an instant."

Josh cycled through all the faces, all the people he had observed during his brief stay on the plane, with his mind reeling thinking about the countless masses that he had witnessed in his short life.

"Feel your life force, your Ki, centered in your abdomen, coursing throughout your body, guided through your meridians, feeding your every organ, every system of your entire body. The combination of your food, water and air, all contribute to provide you with Ki, enabling you to live, to continue your brief transient existence on our planet earth."

Josh could feel the tingle of the vital force travelling throughout his body. His abdomen moving in and out with every breath, firing the furnace of energy located in his energetic center. Tsuyoshi remained silent for some minutes, allowing Josh to truly absorb all that had been said.

"You may now open your eyes, Josh," he said quietly.

Josh opened his eyes again, looking around the cabin with a new respect for his place within it. He returned his chair to an upright position and sat quietly, collecting his thoughts. After some minutes he felt his attention recede, the last tenuous feelings of his expansive body slowly contracting back into himself. Again he was left as a single, solitary man, perceived as separate from his surroundings. Disappointed at his return to 'normal', Josh sighed.

"I can't hold onto that feeling, that knowledge that I just experienced," Josh said.

"A lifetime of learned separation will not evaporate overnight. If you have had any real glimpse of this truth you are indeed fortunate. You then have something to inform your practice, some experience that reminds you of the truth behind our collective longing."

"The truth being that we are all one?" Josh asked.

"Yes," Tsuyoshi answered. "We are each being drawn inexorably back towards this fundamental truth. A truth that lies deep within our bodies, but long forgotten by our minds. This journey may take place over many lifetimes, with countless lessons learned, many missteps taken, all on a meandering journey leading back to what we have always known."

"But how can we forget something so important, so fundamental to our existence?"

"The perpetual distraction of our minds and the dominance of our egos. Look at the animal kingdom. Look at how animals move so effortlessly through their worlds.

You don't see a cat fumble as they leap onto a tall ledge, a bird scared that they will misjudge their landing on the narrow branch of a tree, do you? These beings have never forgotten their sense of unity, they move in accord with the natural world, in accord with the Tao. They are not concerned with themselves or appearances..."

"So why then, why all this? Why do we go through all of this then?"

"How can one really know completeness without first knowing separation?" Tsuyoshi posed. "Before time, there was only the One, the Tao, and everything was good. There was only unity because there was only One. There was no time, because the One was unchanging, complete, and content. But how can the One experience knowledge without the other? When there was only Tao, there was no knowledge. There was no-thing! There was only Tao. It took the magnificence of creation to create everything! Knowledge is born from separation. Experience is born from the other. Time only exists to hold the timeless present, a cradle protecting the most precious stone. From the time of the Big Bang, form has multiplied from formlessness for billions of years. It took this creation of many, of apparent separation, for the One to experience knowing, to experience anything! Before any-thing existed, there was only Tao, there was nothing to experience! Our conscious existence allows the universe to look back on itself in awe. We admire the beauty of our own creation - we created the universe because we are the universe! We are the creation, and we are the creators!"

"We are the universe?" Josh asked, bemused.

"We are all soul bodies on a path towards unification with the source of all things, unity with Tao. It is as natural as breathing to seek unity, it is encoded within every cell of our bodies. We seek unity within our relationships, we yearn for the unity we felt in the womb with our mothers. These drives are often mistaken for our greatest longing, wanting an end to our feelings of separation, the end to duality, unification with the Tao. We feel alone in the world because of separation, we feel that we are isolated, incomplete..."

"But now you're contradicting yourself. You said that there is no separation, and there is only One, but then you refer to us as individuals on a path to experiencing unification... How can that make sense?"

"We take you, Josh Black, to be an individual, a 'one'. And yet, we know you are made up of organs, muscles and bones, which in turn are made up of millions of cells, which are made up of billions of atoms. And yet, you are still one man named 'Josh'.

And you are also an organism among billions on this planet we call earth, all living and interacting together, with everyone affecting everyone else... then there is earth, a small planet holding a moon in orbit with its gravity, but with the moon in turn affecting our oceans. Our sun profoundly affects our solar system, holding all of our surrounding planets in consistent orbit and giving us life through solar energy. And so continues the celestial mechanics of the universe, from stars and planets, to solar systems and galaxies, an intricate flow entwining all. And it all came from a massive explosion of creativity, the same source fourteen and a half billion years ago. Indeed we are all the same source, and the same source is us!"

Josh let his mind drift back from thoughts of the galaxy, down to contemplating his part, his place within the world.

"So if everything is interconnected... and everything affects everything..." he began as a troubling thought arose.

"I almost feel scared to do anything," Josh exclaimed "because of the fear that my actions will cause unintended harm to others!"

"But your refusal to act could also cause such harm," Tsuyoshi cautioned.

"So what do I do?" Josh asked. "If everything affects everything, how can I be responsible for any of my own actions? Aren't they then just caused by the actions of everyone and everything else?"

"A very good question. Living unconsciously, you will indeed be moved through life like the proverbial pawn. But most of us don't realize that we possess the power of the Gods within us, to change the universe as we see fit."

"I don't understand." Josh said.

"As humans, each of us is lit by the divine light, the consciousness of the universe, by God or Allah, the Tao or Yahweh, whatever name you would like to use. Because of this, we have the power, the freedom, to rise above the causal soup we find ourselves in, and command genuine free action. We choose a life of unconsciousness, a life driven by manipulation of our basic instincts, although we are barely aware of doing so. But I'm afraid this ignorance is no excuse, and it is through this pervading unconsciousness that we face the perils that currently threaten us and all other species on our planet. We can all choose to continue our current course, and let the chips fall where they may, or, start to truly live, and move toward the kind of utopic existence that we are taught to only believe is possible in the heavens."

"So an awareness of our freedom, or our current lack of it, can solve all our problems?" Josh asked.

"As our resources become scarcer and our long neglect of our environment wreaks havoc on our globe, all our social problems of today will pail into insignificance with what awaits us tomorrow. But the solution to these problems and the avoidance of this horrific future lie in our collective action, our unified spirit."

"But I think we all already know that Tsuyoshi, and it hasn't brought us closer to actually doing anything about it!"

"I don't know if I totally agree. Yes, we have realizations forced upon us every day, lessons constantly presented throughout our lives, but it is our free choice how we react to them. You chose to seek out Zach when you were confronted with the futility of your former life path. You could have chosen to ignore your inner drive and lived out a life filled with pain and disappointment. Or, you could choose to walk the direction in which you have chosen. Your journey is analogous to the journey of mankind. We are forced daily towards the realization of the collective failure of our current path. We may choose to ignore this, leading down a path of further misery, sorrow and bloodshed, or we can break free of our past and forge another road, another way..."

"So we are all responsible for the violent world we now live in then?" Josh asked.

"Do I think the violence and wars perpetrated around the globe are heinous? Yes. Are these things my responsibility? Only insofar as my actions and decisions caused them. Often people bemoan the state of the world, the actions of others, the follies of humanity. They can see every misstep of our forefathers, all the misdeeds of their fellow man. However, sudden myopia often develops when their piercing insight is applied against the thing that they hold undeniable responsibility for... their own actions. We all have a unique responsibility for our own actions. If we could each curtail our corrupting desires and let our best selves shine forth, would we collectively be in the trouble that we find ourselves? Of course not!"

"But isn't part of the reason we that know what we know because of the horrible choices we have made as a species?" Josh asked.

Tsuyoshi nodded his head. "Excellent, Josh," he began. "All our violence, our hate, our pain, has indeed created the fertile ground we now find for true peace. Are we all ready to embrace this?

Are we ready to accept peace? We can all choose this now for ourselves and thus, the world. Are we willing to set aside all the malevolent prejudices we shamefully harbor in the recesses of our soul and live in true peace? Pain and suffering are powerful agents for change, for transformation. But these no longer need to be experienced firsthand to be effective. We have built up a library of tales of death and destruction to serve the world for peace, to help teach the soul love and forgiveness, enough to last our civilization for thousands of years!"

"Okay then, so which is it? Do we have a shared destiny, moving towards 'unification', or, are we truly free agents, each making choices that will decide if we can live in peace together or destroy ourselves?"

"Both statements you made Josh are true, although I don't think humanity will destroy itself quite yet. We are quite a resilient organism, in case you hadn't noticed! We each make our choices as we walk through our many lives, each time forging our own path through the darkness. But regardless of the journey taken, the destination of unity is the same for all. It is like we are all explorers looking to climb a colossal mountain. There are numerous ways to the top, all filled with different trials and tribulations, but all have the same final destination… the glorious summit… promising a vista of unimaginable beauty. Josh, I speak of the special time we now find ourselves in, because we now have a real possibility of moving into a future governed by the transcendence of the spirit. We no longer need to learn lessons from global violence and grief, we no longer need to experience such tremendous pain. We have forgotten our birthright as observers of bliss, as those that are here to chronicle the magnificence of the universe. We can straddle the paradox of separation and unity, experiencing both simultaneously! We can all feel the contentment of never being alone, our senses extending to feel a part of everything that is, but also experience the transient joys that separation entails, reveling in all the excitement and adventure of our brief, unique lives. My heart truly aches for humanity because we are so close to ending so much pain and ushering in a time of unbridled joy. I just hope we can feel this soon…"

Tsuyoshi clasped his hands in front of his chest tapping his thumbs together and stared intently at Josh.

"Thomas Jefferson held greater weight in his words than he realized when he said, 'Enlighten the people, generally, and tyranny and oppressions of body and mind will vanish like spirits at the dawn of day'."

Tsuyoshi paused a moment, allowing Josh to fully absorb the words of the third American President.

"The influence of enlightened masters like Jesus, Mohammad and the Buddha resonate throughout history, with their spiritual truths inspiring millions. Imagine if we had millions of enlightened beings on our globe at once? Imagine if those spiritually realized were celebrated like the athletes and celebrities of today? If we all, as a globe took to the task of seeking authentic spiritual experience? If science truly turned its unbiased attentions to the spiritual? When enough of us come to realize the depth and wonder that waits dormant inside us all, everything will change. That is why seekers like yourself are the primary architects of this joyous future for all."

"But I'm not going to save the world! I've barely started this path and I'm not sure I could inspire anyone to do anything!" Josh exclaimed.

"It's only through collective action that our world will change. Life is not a Hollywood blockbuster. A lone action hero does not save the world from destruction. As for being an inspiration, living an authentic life and following a regular spiritual practice will have numerous benefits for yourself that you'll feel internally, with this in turn affecting the lives of those around you and in the greater community in ways you cannot imagine."

"But people don't have the time to train like I have over the past months. Like it or not, people have to work..."

"For now, yes they do. But great things are all accomplished in small pieces of time, spread out over time. Small changes in individual behavior will help lay the groundwork for this spiritual revolution. For example, the world would be in a much better state if people were to contemplate two things every day. Upon awakening, ponder their impending death. We are taught to avoid facing this undeniable truth. However, we all know that death is coming nearer to us with each waking moment. Bravely facing this knowledge can serve as a catalyst to make the most of the upcoming day – to truly be present in our actions and use our limited time wisely. Then before sleeping, one should look up at the night's sky and ponder the sheer scale of the universe before them, and their size in comparison to it. One's worldly concerns and problems pale into insignificance if one can come close to comprehending this vastness."

"I could see how that could help," Josh agreed.

"Our obsession with instant gratification, our demands of immediate satisfaction, both contribute greatly to our current global dilemmas. However, within these problematic drives lies the key to our collective salvation. The obsession with now can lead us into a deep appreciation of the present.

We needn't be compelled to dull our senses, to feel emotionless in our present. We need only accept that this is all that will ever exist for us and that we access our whole world from this moment. When we have integrated this fact into our consciousness, we will arrive home – and we can begin to live our lives. Staying present throughout your day grants you the real freedom to choose the course of your life."

"But what about formal training?"

"What about it? Formal training is very important. You have seen the huge benefits it can bring you in a short period of time. In this age of choice we have access to a spiritual supermarket, with innumerable paths open to us. Everything you have been exposed to - meditation, Qi Gong, yoga - are all now available right across the world. Practitioners would be living all around you, but if you are not aware of these possibilities you would remain ignorant of this. This is where the lives of seekers like yourself can have such a positive impact on others. If one has been fortunate enough to have been presented with this knowledge, these practices, these experiences, one has the unique opportunity to participate in helping catalyze the next era of humanity, the true age of enlightenment. Just twenty minutes a day of formal practice is enough to revolutionize your life and contribute to the salvation of the planet. But what you'll often find that as a result of these twenty minutes, you'll feel so good that you'll find more time to practice. Just like going to the gym for the body, one must also train the mind and the soul."

"Is it really that easy?" Josh asked.

"Yes, it is! You just need to seek, and then put in the time. Look at your recent experience. In an effort to find your friend you were brought into contact with spiritual teachers of different walks of life, all able to provide you with guidance, all able to help you move closer to experiencing your divinity, to experience the unity of all things, all helping you to experience purpose. Let's face it, without purpose in our lives, what's the point?"

Josh's mind wandering back over the experiences he had in the months prior, he was again filled with a sense of wonder. A purposeful existence that he had unknowingly sought for so long had been magically handed to him. How could all this exist in the world, all around him, and he remain ignorant of it?

He answered his own question by reflecting on his previously skewed perception: to his former self, none of these possibilities did exist!

"I can appreciate what you're saying. I haven't felt like that for years."

"We are so spoilt now. We have genuine spiritual teachers of all levels littered throughout our cities, waiting to provide us with guidance. We have access to resources like massive online bookstores that can provide anyone, anywhere with translations of innumerable spiritual treatises. So many of these texts were only available to initiates of esoteric groups in the past, only revealed to students after many years of arduous service. The rise of the internet grants access to an unfathomable amount of knowledge to all corners of our planet. Previously unimaginable volumes of information are now available at the touch of a button. So even if you are isolated from any teacher, you still have access to the words of past great sages. Those who may be alone but spiritually brave can still forge their own path with help from voices of the past."

Josh turned away from Tsuyoshi, staring into space in front of him. He could feel the simultaneous promise of the world that was being created and the potential for unmitigated disaster. The fragility of the entire human enterprise was more apparent to him than ever before, and yet he was now equally aware of the tremendous power for good, for change, for spiritual empowerment that each of us carried within ourselves. He took a few deep breaths and brought his mind back to the present moment, turning again towards Tsuyoshi.

"So, what do I do now?" Josh asked.

The craving for guidance, for direction evident in his eyes, Tsuyoshi felt tremendous compassion for Josh. He could see he had finally realized the path that was before him. The path that was before us all. He spoke the only words suitable at that moment in time.

"Josh, you are free to do whatever you like," Tsuyoshi responded.

"It's your choice..."

Thank you for taking this journey with me,
I trust you found something valuable. I look forward
to connecting with you online soon.

web simonboylan.com
email info@simonboylan.com
twitter.com/simonboylan
facebook.com/taoofsimonboylan
pinterest.com/simonboylan

We are all creating the world of tomorrow…
Are you consciously creating your part?